Just One More Moment

The Kingston Family
(The Sterling Family)
Book 1

NEW YORK TIMES BESTSELLING AUTHOR
Carly Phillips

Copyright © Karen Drogin 2024
Published by CP Publishing
Print Edition

Cover Photo: Wander Aguiar
Cover Design: Maria @steamydesigns
Editing: Rumi Khan and Claire Milto: BB Virtual Assistant for Authors

* * *

JUST ONE MORE MOMENT

She thinks *happily ever after* only happens in romance novels.

He can't *wait* to prove her wrong...

Falling in love is *not* on Raven Walsh's agenda. Running from her past keeps her way too busy for *that*. She can, however, handle a friends-with-benefits scenario with the hot billionaire who co-owns The Back Door bar. But trusting him with her heart? Not a chance...

Remington Sterling has had his eye on the smart and sexy Raven since she started waitressing at his bar. He knows she's gun-shy where relationships are concerned. But he's ready to do *whatever* it takes to convince her he's worth the risk...

When Raven's secrets catch up to her in a *big* way, she must decide if the potential cost of trusting Remy is more than she's willing to pay—and Remy will need to figure out how far he's willing to go for love...

Just One More Moment, book 1 in the Sterling Family series (all can be read as standalones), is a spicy contemporary romance featuring a ready-to-run heroine and the possessive, protective alpha hero who is *more* than ready to catch her.

Chapter One

"I NOW PRONOUNCE you husband and wife. You may kiss the—" Before the officiant could finish his sentence, Zach Dare swept his bride into his arms and dipped her head for a long, nearly-inappropriate-for-an-audience kiss.

Raven Walsh joined the rest of the guests, clapping for the newlyweds as they joined hands and made their way back down the white rose lined aisle.

"I adore a good second-chance love story," Stevie Palmer, Raven's friend and waitress at the bar she managed, said. Stevie rose from her seat and Raven followed suit, waiting for everyone in their row to file out and head for the reception.

Raven laughed. "You and your romance novels." She shook her head at her book-loving friend. "But in this case, I have to say I agree." Even she, with the lack of a relationship in her life, couldn't deny these two deserved happiness and a long future together. "If anyone was meant to be together, it's Zach and Hadley." They'd lost each other once due to circumstances beyond their control and fought hard upon Hadley's return. In more ways than one.

1

The bridal party, consisting of Hadley's young sister, and all seven of Zach's brothers, sisters, and sisters-in-law, followed the couple down the aisle. So did the best man, Zach's best friend and business partner.

He also happened to be Raven's boss and the star of her fantasies. Wearing a black, double-breasted tuxedo with wide lapels, a white shirt, and black bow tie, Remington Sterling was the epitome of sexy. His brown hair was lightly gelled. Choosing not to shave, he'd kept the beard she loved and imagined scraping along her thighs. Which would not be happening. *Bad, Raven.* She shouldn't be having naughty thoughts about her boss.

He might flirt up a storm whenever they were together but as much as she wanted to know him better, and end up between the sheets, Raven had to keep her distance. Her past was always waiting to pop up and destroy anyone she got close to. These days, that past was getting closer than ever. She shuddered and pushed the thought out of her mind.

Remy walked up the aisle and stood parallel to her row. He caught her gaze, treating her to a wink before striding forward, leaving her with a view of his broad shoulders and back, and a tingling feeling low in her belly.

Beside her, Stevie let out a whistle. "That man

wants you."

And Raven wanted him.

Too bad she wasn't destined for the happily ever after Hadley had found. Raven didn't begrudge her friend the love she and Zach shared. She just wished one day, she could have the same. But fate didn't seem to cut her any breaks. Still, she'd created a good life for herself and wasn't one to dwell on the negatives.

The people beside her started to move and Raven followed the woman next to her out of the row. A little while later, she and Stevie stood with a glass in hand, looking around the Meridian NYC Hotel room where the cocktail hour was being held.

"I have to say, this drink is delicious." Raven took another sip of the wedding couple's specialty offering, a peppermint white Russian, made with Kahlua, her favorite liqueur.

"Rich people and their signature drinks," Stevie said. "My brother got married at the VFW Hall in my small New Hampshire town. Guests paid for their own alcohol. I'm sure you get it, right?"

Raven stilled mid-sip. For all outward appearances, she was just like Stevie. A New York City working girl. Her clothing was a mix of thrift store finds and affordable fashion, she shopped at inexpensive grocery stores and ate at home more often than she spent money in restaurants. When she did go out, she knew all the good but cheap places and her recreation choices were the same. Free museum days, outdoor art in the summer, and free movies at Backyard at Hudson Yards.

Her upbringing, however, was the same as Remy's. Private schools, expensive restaurants, summers in Sag Harbor...

"Raven?"

She shook her head. "Sorry," she said to her friend. "I got lost in thought."

"I was saying I'm sure you understand how out of place I feel at this wedding. The Back Door is much more my speed."

Raven leaned over the table so she could talk lower and still be heard. "Actually, I grew up like this." She gestured around the gorgeously decorated room.

"You're kidding?" Stevie's eyes opened wide.

Raven shook her head. "My biological mom died when I was five and I went into foster care. I was quickly adopted by a wealthy family and had all... this." And so much more, she thought with a shiver.

Stevie raised her eyebrows. "But you're so unaffected."

Raven laughed. "Much to my mother's chagrin. She wanted a frilly, girly girl. Instead, she got me."

Stepping back, Stevie looked her over. "Well, if she saw you in that dress, she'd rethink her assessment, at least on the surface." She lifted her glass to her red-stained lips and took a sip. "And if Remy's stares are anything to go by, he also likes what he sees."

Pleasure rushed through Raven at the thought. No matter how many times she pretended to ignore the man's flirting and innuendos, she enjoyed it nonetheless. If she weren't always on edge, waiting for her psychotic brother to be released from prison, she'd want nothing more than to indulge in everything Remington Sterling.

"Where did you find the gown?" Stevie asked. "After searching everywhere, I had to settle for plain black. It was the only one I liked."

Raven placed her glass on the table and smoothed her hands over her floor-length dress. "Would you believe I found it in a consignment store? And you look incredible. Black always works."

Raven might come from money but her mother had cut her off for reasons she had no desire to think about. Even if she had access to the family money, she couldn't see the point in spending a fortune on a dress she'd probably only wear once.

"Good job! That color is incredible."

The turquoise gown had stood out among the black ones, calling to her, and once she'd tried it on, she'd been sold. The blue-green hue complemented her skin tone and she'd loved the look of the halter top that dipped low at her cleavage.

She turned and looked over her shoulder to find Remy standing with a deep amber-colored drink in his hand. He talked with Asher Dare, Zach's oldest brother, but his gaze was on Raven. In all the time she'd worked for him, spent time with him at the bar, and tried not to react to his flirting, he'd never looked at her quite this way before.

From the heated expression on his face, the deep flush highlighting his cheekbones, and the way his golden-brown eyes that matched the color of his whiskey drank her in, Stevie was right. He appreciated what he saw.

Stevie tapped her shoulder and Raven turned. "Oops. Sorry." Raven blushed at being caught staring at her boss.

Her friend grinned. "Why does something tell me I'm going to be leaving this wedding alone?" They'd done their makeup and dressed at her apartment and had taken an Uber to the party together. When the night ended, they'd planned to split the car service, Raven getting dropped off first, then Stevie.

Raven shook her head. "I wouldn't do that to you," she said, her stare still on Remy.

He said something to Asher before making his way toward her with a predatory look in his eyes.

Stevie chuckled. "Famous last words, my friend. Famous last words."

Chapter Two

REMY GLANCED AROUND the rose-filled room and knew the décor was courtesy of Zach's mom, Serenity. All Hadley and Zach cared about was getting married and starting their lives together. Remy liked Hadley for his friend. She was as down-to-earth as a person could be. Sort of like Raven.

His gaze drifted to the woman who was never far from his thoughts. She stood with one of the bar waitresses and they talked as they sipped their drinks.

Remy was used to seeing Raven wearing her Back Door uniform; a pair of formfitting black jeans and a matching T-shirt with the bar logo on the back. Though she was tall and thin, her round breasts filled out the snug shirt and her jeans accentuated the sweet curve of her ass. She typically wore her long hair up in a ponytail on workdays and when he ran into her on days off, her light brown curls fell to her mid-back.

He'd thought she was gorgeous with a full face of makeup and casual clothes, but he hadn't been prepared for the siren who showed up tonight. The turquoise dress accentuated her green eyes and draped her body, the low dip at her cleavage revealing what her T-shirts only hinted at.

He itched to unwind her hair now pulled into an updo. Then he'd thread his fingers through the soft strands, wrap it around his hand, and pull hard as he entered her from behind. Imagining the moans coming from deep in her throat, he thought about flipping her over so he could look into those teal-colored eyes and watch her face as she came.

She was so fucking hot but more than that, she had a good heart. How did he know? He'd seen her take a sandwich in hand each night and walk it out to the homeless man who all but owned the corner nearby. From the time he'd bought into Zach's two businesses and met Raven, he'd been hooked.

"You haven't heard a word I've said, have you?" Asher asked.

Caught, Remy forced his gaze away from Raven and glanced at Zach's brother. "Not a word."

Asher shook his head and laughed. "Nothing I can say, considering I've been in your shoes." He looked around the room, finally locking his gaze on his young wife, Nikki. "Hell, I still am," he admitted.

Asher and Nikki's story was unusual. He'd taken his now wife to his Bahamas retreat as a favor to his best friend as a means of getting her away from a nude photo scandal. Since Nikki was much younger, not to mention his friend's little sister, Asher had tried to keep his hands off. Needless to say, he hadn't. It had taken a while, but they were now a solid couple.

Remy's gaze came to rest on Raven again, watching her toy with a strand of hair dangling around her face.

"Oh, hell. Go for it already," Asher muttered on a low chuckle.

With a shrug, Remy decided his friend had a point. It was time. His stare still locked with Raven's, he made his way across the room and joined the two women standing by a high table.

"Hello, ladies," he said, his focus never wavering.

"Hi, boss," Stevie replied.

He glanced her way and smiled. "I think you can call me Remy when we're not at work."

She laughed. "Remy," she parroted. "Since you're here, can you keep Raven company while I go to the ladies' room?"

He turned to see Raven glare at her friend and stifled a laugh. "Go ahead, Stevie. I'd be more than happy to take care of her."

Stevie's devilish grin told him she was playing matchmaker. Remy was so grateful he might even give her a raise.

He waited for the other woman to walk off before stepping closer to his prey. "You look beautiful tonight," he said to Raven.

Edible, but telling her that would be beyond inappropriate. Not that he cared much for proprieties but he didn't want to scare her off.

"Thank you." Her eyes did a sweep of his body, ending with her gaze meeting his. "You're looking dashing yourself."

He grinned, pleased she wasn't shy or backing away. "Thank you." He took a sip of his drink and placed it on the table.

"I see the men have a signature drink as well. What's in yours?" she asked.

"Whiskey smash. It's whiskey with mint and powdered sugar sprinkled on top. Jury's still out. I prefer my liquor neat. What's yours called?" He pointed to the two glasses that were hers and Stevie's.

"Peppermint white Russian." Picking up a glass, Raven took a long taste and let out a groan of delight. One that had his cock perking up in his tuxedo pants. "Delicious."

"Mmm. I'd like a taste," he said, staring at her mouth because he wanted to sample the liqueur directly from her lips.

Her eyes grew heavy at his implication. "Here." She offered him her glass instead.

Since it was the next best thing and her lips had already been on the rim, he accepted the drink and lifted it to his mouth. With their stares still connected, he drank. The thick, coffee liqueur mixed with vodka—Dirty Dare Vodka, no doubt—was sweet. "I agree. It's delicious." He placed the glass back on the table.

The lights began to flash, indicating they were ready to move on to the ballroom part of the night.

"Time to take our seats. I'll see you later," Raven said, the relief in her voice palpable. She started to walk away but Remy was onto her.

He caught up and hooked his arm in hers as they stepped toward the ballroom along with the rest of the guests.

"What are you doing?" she asked.

"Escorting you to our table." He guided her around the slower people who had stopped to talk. "You're at table two and so am I."

She tripped and he steadied her, keeping her close. "Aren't you sitting with the wedding party?" she asked.

"Nope."

He felt her stare and turned to wink at her before continuing to guide them to their destination. He'd asked Hadley to put them at the same table.

"Don't worry. Stevie's sitting with us, too." It was natural that she and Stevie, and anyone else from work, would be together.

Hadley had originally put him with the Dares but when she'd shown him the seating chart, he'd noticed the work table was smaller than the normal ten-person round. He'd gladly offered to sit there. Zach's soon-to-be wife had treated him to a knowing look and a pleased smile. Then she'd asked if his willingness had anything to do with Raven.

He'd answered her with one word. *Everything.* His seating choice was all about the woman beside him now.

They stepped into the large room and even Remy was overwhelmed by the sight. The tables had high, white rose centerpieces, and the lighting gave the space a light lavender glow.

"This looks… beautiful," Raven murmured, obviously in awe.

Which surprised him considering she came from a wealthy family. Remy only knew as much about Raven as Zach's hiring background check told him. The most curious fact was that her given name was Caroline Kane, yet she went by Raven Walsh. He had no idea why.

Raven was a gorgeous blend of contradictions he wanted to understand even more than he plain wanted her. She lived in the apartment upstairs from the bar and Zach mentioned she'd asked him to put an alarm system on the windows and doors before she'd moved in. Not that he blamed her, being a single woman living alone in Manhattan. But as a former detective and current private investigator, it sparked his curiosity.

Raven Walsh was a mystery. And Remy liked mysteries.

"The décor is beautiful," she said.

He leaned in close and whispered in her ear, "Not as beautiful as you."

Her lips parted and the sight had him desperate for a taste but before he could make a move, someone jostled them, killing the moment.

"Sorry," a female voice said as the person rushed around them.

A flush stained Raven's cheeks. He understood. His entire body vibrated with need, but he sucked it up and led her to the table he'd scoped out earlier. One set away from the speakers and near the dance floor, a place where he intended to take Raven into his arms and pull her tight against his body for the first time.

Most of the guests had claimed their seats, including Stevie, who stood beside her chair and waved at Raven. Remy released her arm and she rushed over to her friend, placing her purse on her chair.

Remy took his time walking over because there was just one seat left at the table.

And it was right next to Raven.

IF RAVEN DIDN'T know better, she'd say Remy had planned the seating, from them being at the same table to him ending up sitting beside her. They'd taken their chairs, waiting for the bride and groom to make their entrance, and Raven studied Remy's profile.

A waiter walked around the table, filling champagne glasses, and Raven decided to stop worrying and just enjoy a fun evening. Her other boss, a man she admired, had married the love of his life. The band played dance music that had her tapping her foot to the beat.

She picked up the glass and drank the bubbly liquid, aware that she easily got drunk on good champagne. So she nodded when the waiter asked if she wanted a refill and let the music fill her soul. Beside her, Stevie bobbed her head to the familiar chorus of the song while the man on Remy's other side had engaged him in conversation.

Once they rose to welcome the bride and groom, the band grew louder and Stevie cheered. "Let's dance!"

Finishing her third glass, Raven put the flute on the table and rose to her feet. "Let's go!"

Lightheaded in the best way, her mood now high, they made their way to the crowded center of the floor and found an empty space. They shimmied and danced to the music, surrounded by other single women who rocked along with them. After a while, the music slowed, and Raven realized she was thirsty.

She felt his presence before she saw him. A warmth at her back and a firm hand on her waist as Remy turned her toward him. Stevie, Remy noted, had already walked back to their table.

"Dance with me." It wasn't a question.

She placed one hand on his shoulder. Before she could do the same with her other, he pulled her against him, winding his arms around her waist. The move forced her to do the same and she wrapped her arms around his neck.

Their bodies came into contact and there was no missing the hard ridge of his erection as they swayed to the music. Her sex pulsed with need and she felt her arousal soak her panties. A low growl reverberated through his chest and she couldn't deny how much this man got to her.

"You have no idea how long I've wanted to feel you in my arms." His low voice rumbled in her ear. "But you've been playing hard to get."

Tipping her head, she met his gaze. "That's because I am," she said, unable to hide her grin.

He laughed and she felt his body shake. "Then it's a good thing I not only like a challenge, but I'm damn good at getting what I want."

"Whatever you say, big man." And he was. To her

five-foot-four, he towered over her at over six feet. But wrapped in his arms, she felt protected.

Watch it, Raven. Remember this isn't meant to get serious.

He splayed his large hand across her bare back and it was all she could do not to moan at the warm, arousing touch.

Telling herself it was just a dance, not a commitment, she placed her head on his shoulder and allowed herself time to just be.

She breathed in deep, taking in his familiar sandalwood and musk scent. Whenever she passed by him at work, she would inhale on purpose, just to get a sniff, he smelled so good. If she had her way, she'd spray it on her pillow and breathe it in all night. No doubt she'd have erotic dreams of him if she did.

"Okay, ladies and gentlemen! Time to take your seats and start dinner," the band leader said.

The rest of the evening passed quickly with good food, good friends, and a healthy dose of arousal with Remy by her side. He was a total gentleman, talking to the people at their table, but his focus was on her.

After dessert, when she thought she was home free, he rose from his seat and extended a hand. "One last dance," he said. Again, not a question but an assumption she'd say yes.

And she did, standing, accepting his hand and letting him lead her back to the dance floor. This time, they came together naturally, moving in sync and silence. He held her close, and her body tingled with awareness and her panties were done for.

The band leader announced the last song and they began to play a final fun dance number. Instead of leading her to her seat where her purse was, he pulled her to a corner of the room far from the speakers, instruments, and noise.

"What's wrong?" she asked.

"Nothing. Tonight, everything has been right." He placed a hand beneath her chin and tilted her head so she met his gaze. "Do you agree?"

She swallowed hard. Looking into his whiskey-colored eyes, she found it impossible to argue. "I do."

He lowered his head slowly, giving her every opportunity to stop the inevitable, but they'd been building toward this all evening and she wanted this. So much. And then his mouth was on hers, warm, soft, and gentler than she'd imagined he'd be. He moved his lips back and forth, as if savoring their first kiss. Completely on board, she kissed him back, wrapping her arms around his neck and hanging on while he parted her lips and his tongue met hers.

A low groan rumbled through him and she rose onto her toes to take more. She wasn't sure how long they stood in the corner, wrapped in each other, unaware of anyone or anything else until finally, he braced his hands on her hips and lifted his head.

Oxygen returned to her brain and suddenly she realized what they'd done. A quick glance around told her nobody was watching and she blew out a relieved breath. But even if they'd been caught making out like teenagers, she couldn't regret the stolen moment.

"That was better than I imagined it would be," he said, a hazy fog of desire in his gaze.

"And have you imagined us kissing?" She wanted desperately to hear his answer.

"Every night of the week."

Surprise rippled through her at his reply. She looked at him, expecting his patented, sexy grin. Instead, his expression was serious as he held out his hand. "Come upstairs with me?"

This time he *asked,* and if anything would break through the walls she tried to keep high, that kiss and giving her a choice had done it. After what she'd been through in the past, telling her they'd dance was one thing. Informing her they'd be going upstairs to his room, quite another.

Remy had proven he was smart enough to read her needs and show he respected her choices. She found that, along with his alpha-like tendencies, hot as hell.

Finally, his question registered. "You booked a room?" She was surprised considering he had an apartment farther downtown.

He shook his head. "But I do have connections." He winked at her and dammit, she was charmed by him. "*And,* if you say yes, I sure as hell don't want to take the time to get my car and drive us to my place." He reached out to tuck a stray strand of hair behind her ear.

The brush of his fingertips against her cheek had her trembling and her nipples hardened beneath her flimsy halter dress. The one that didn't allow her to wear a bra.

"We'd be so good together, Raven."

Yes. Yes, they would be, she thought, and swayed toward him as he spoke, his deep voice beckoning to her baser instincts.

She'd been fighting her attraction to him for so long, too afraid to get close to him. To anyone, really. But tonight he'd demolished her walls and she'd allowed herself to want something that in the long run, she couldn't have.

But didn't she deserve this one night of pleasure?

She couldn't imagine him wanting more, either. He wasn't the type of man to flaunt his affairs. In the time since he'd bought into the bar, she'd never seen him with a woman or heard him mention a serious girl-friend. She'd come to the conclusion that he was probably a one-night stand kind of guy, which worked in her favor.

"Raven."

His gruff voice broke into her thoughts. "Is the decision that difficult?" he asked.

It really wasn't. She shook her head in reply.

"Is that a yes?" he asked and she nodded.

Before she could process her decision, he grabbed her hand and walked them back to the table so she could retrieve her bag. Although she wanted to say good night to the happy couple, they were surrounded by family with no way for Raven and Remy to get close.

They agreed to make their apologies later and soon he'd led her to the lobby, booked a room, and they'd taken a crowded elevator to the sixteenth floor.

When he'd asked her to come upstairs, she told herself it was one night. One she deserved, since she hadn't been with any man in way too long and she *knew* sex with Remy would be incredible.

But as he slid the key card into the door and she heard the click, she was forced to admit there was more going on between them than just sex. He'd kept one hand on her since she'd agreed to join him tonight, maintaining the connection she'd begun to feel on the dance floor and that he'd solidified with a kiss she'd felt down to her toes.

Remy made her feel wanted and that was something sorely lacking in Raven's life. But as much as she liked the warm, gooey feelings sliding around in her body and her mind, she warned herself that all she could have was this one night. So she intended to make the most of it.

Chapter Three

REMY WAS MORE in tune with Raven than she realized. With his heart in his throat, he'd watched her hesitancy as he waited for her to decide whether to come upstairs with him. Now that she had, he wasn't going to tread lightly. The worst thing he could do was give her the chance to think… and run. He needed her engaged and with him the whole way.

He let them into the hotel room and the door slammed shut behind them. He tossed the key onto the dresser, turned and saw her looking around the luxurious room before her gaze landed on him. Aware of her captivated stare, he shrugged off his tuxedo jacket and laid it over the nearest chair, then undid the bow tie, slid one side around and off his neck, and placed it beside the key card. Cuff links came next.

All the while, she watched, her lips slightly parted, her cheeks flushed with desire. He undid his cuffs before releasing each button on the shirt until the garment hung open at his sides. Her stare came to rest on his bare chest.

Yeah. She was all in. He crossed the room to where she stood, braced his hands on her hips, and yanked her against him, the hard length of his erection rubbing against her stomach.

"Remy," she said on a moan.

His name on her lips had his cock standing at attention, wanting out of the confines of his pants. "I'm all yours, sweetheart."

Her eyes dilated at the endearment, and she grasped his lapels, clearly wanting to take off his shirt. Helping, he shrugged it down his shoulders and onto the floor.

She reached for the opening of his trousers but he grasped her hands, stopping her before she could release him.

She pursed her lips in a pretty pout. "But I want to see."

He grinned. "And you will. But I want my fill of you first." And if she touched him, he might just come in her hand. "Turn around," he said, his voice as gravelly as he'd ever heard it, desire a live pulsing being in his veins.

She did as he asked and with her hair already up, he easily leaned in, breathing in her delicate peach scent. Closing his eyes, he savored being so close to what he wanted. He pressed his lips to her soft skin before flicking open the clasp and easing the gown off her body, leaving her in a pair of tiny silk panties and high silver heeled sandals. Her skin was flawless, a creamy vision that had him pulling in a deep, calming breath.

She turned to face him, giving him his first look at her perfect breasts. Not more than a handful, which had allowed her to ditch the bra, she was his fantasy come to life and he sealed his lips over hers.

She moaned and their tongues tangled, giving him the go-ahead. And when she slid her fingers into his hair, holding him in place, his heart slammed hard inside his chest.

He walked her backward until her back hit the wall. He took in her heavy-lidded gaze, then pulled one of her legs up so she cradled his dick, his solid erection rubbing against her pussy. Her breathing changed, small pants along with little gasps, so he moved faster, giving her what she needed. He wanted to watch as she came apart before he was too far gone to see. He needed that connection with her, something that showed him this was more than just hot sex, though it was that.

Lifting his hand, he cupped one breast in his palm and worked her nipple with his thumb and forefinger, pinching and releasing the tight bud. And she began to writhe against him, harder and faster, her urgency feeding his desire.

"Take what you need," he coaxed her, rubbing his cock against her covered sex.

"Oh God, so good. More," she demanded. He pinched her nipple hard and she let go, rocking against him, her body trembling as her climax neared.

Knowing he was about to come in his slacks, he replaced his cock with his palm and rubbed the heel of his hand against her soaked panties, giving her pressure and friction, until she shattered.

"Remy!" She screamed his name and her orgasm rushed over her, her hands gripping his shoulders, her nails digging into his skin.

He watched her come, her cheeks flushed, lips damp and parted. Fuck, she was gorgeous.

When her tremors subsided, he stepped back and unhooked his pants, stripping them off along with his boxer shorts, his stiff cock finally free. Precome beaded on the head. Pulling in a harsh breath, he gripped the base tight and groaned at the sensation that rushed through him. In an attempt to stave off a premature orgasm, he forced himself to count to ten and not think about the beautiful woman he'd just made come.

When he opened his lids, he saw Raven staring, eyes wide… panties and shoes off, leaving her completely nude. Ready for him.

He stepped forward and sealed his lips over hers, causing her head to hit the wall and a giggle to escape.

"Sorry, sweetheart. You okay?" he asked.

"Not yet… but I will be." She slid her hands between them and nudged his arm away so she could encircle his cock with her smaller hand, clasping him as best she could.

He set his jaw, letting her have her way, and she pumped her hand up and down his shaft, swiping her thumb over the sensitive head.

"Enough," he gritted out. "Unless you want this to end without my cock inside you."

"Not a chance," she said and immediately released her grip.

He lifted her leg, giving himself access to that sweet pussy, but just as he rubbed himself at her entrance she stilled.

"Condom," she reminded him.

He reared back in surprise. Shit. He'd never wanted anyone badly enough to forget protection. Bending down, he grabbed his pants, found his wallet in a pocket, and pulled out a condom. "Two," he said as he revealed both in his hand.

Once he'd covered himself, he repositioned them, grabbing her leg and setting himself at her entrance once more. He met her gaze and saw a hint of vulnerability there, one he'd never associated with Raven, and an unfamiliar pang squeezed his chest.

Tonight he'd seen glimpses of the real woman behind the professional façade she normally kept in place. She joked with him, stood up to him, and shown him raw emotion. And he liked it. All things he'd have to think about later because she raised her hips and he thrust deep, stilling inside her.

The warmth and sweetness of her pussy enveloped him and he took a moment to savor the tight grip of her sex, the warmth of her body. And the need for her alone. He brushed a kiss over her lips before he began to move, sliding out and plunging back in.

They were joined in an explosion of need. She met each thrust, taking all he had and giving back in return. Over and over, he drove into her, need spiraling inside him. His balls drew up and his spine tingled. He was about to come, something he wouldn't let happen until she climaxed first.

Remembering how she'd come before, he cupped one breast in his hand and tweaked her nipple hard. She shook, rubbing herself against him each time he slammed deep, and then she stilled, moaned, and came apart in his arms.

Two more thrusts and he joined her, rocking her against the wall until his legs felt like Jell-O and it was hard to hold her up along with himself. Still inside her, he focused on getting his breathing to regulate so he could take off the condom and get them into bed.

He lifted his forehead off hers and met her gaze, unable to read her expression. Was she with him or feeling regret?

Before he could ask if she was okay, she grabbed his face in her hands and kissed him full on the lips. And the world as he knew it tilted on its axis.

RAVEN DIDN'T SLEEP. It wasn't because she and Remy had stumbled into bed for a repeat performance, though they had. And it wasn't because she'd let herself indulge in all things Remy Sterling. No, she tossed and turned beside him because of that kiss she'd given him while he was still inside her after their first time.

She'd gone into this wanting to chalk the whole night up to a one-time thing but that kiss and the expression on his face told her he had real feelings. And so did she. Too bad she couldn't let herself enjoy them.

She sighed and glanced at his handsome profile. He breathed in and out, sleeping easily. But he didn't have a past that was going to return and destroy the life he'd built. Raven's sociopath brother might be in prison now but he wouldn't stay there forever. The last thing he'd said after she testified against him was, *I'll get even.* And Lance never said anything he didn't mean.

She'd already moved twice after he'd sent men who'd gotten out of prison before him to stop by and reiterate his warning. Lance meant business and she couldn't risk having feelings for *anyone*. Because if her brother figured out she cared for someone, that she had a weakness, he'd hurt them in order to get to Raven. He'd done it once before.

And the last person she wanted hurt was Remy.

This whole night had probably been one big error in judgment and though she couldn't bring herself to regret it, she couldn't repeat it, either.

Her chest was heavy as she contemplated leaving before he woke up, but she was stronger than that. The least she could do was face him after such a spectacular night. Besides, she'd have to see him at work on Monday anyway, she thought and let out a sigh.

"I can hear you thinking," Remy said, his voice deep and amused.

He wouldn't be if he knew what she'd been considering. She pushed herself up and leaned against the pillows and headboard, pulling the sheet over her breasts.

"No need to hide, sweetheart. I've already seen… and tasted all of you."

Her cheeks burned at the memory of him doing exactly that. "Listen, Remy. Last night was amazing but—"

"No buts. We had fun. Don't overthink things. Okay?"

All she did was overthink, Raven thought.

She met his gaze and was struck hard by how sexy he looked with his extra morning scruff and mussed hair. The desire to run her fingers through the light sprinkling of hair on his chest was strong but she refrained.

She managed a nod. If he was going to take things so lightly, it made it easier for her to, as well. Though, with the way he was studying her through narrowed eyes, and knowing he had a shrewd personality, she wasn't one hundred percent sure she believed his nonchalance.

But she'd go with it. "Good. I'm glad we agree." She removed the sheet and slid out of the bed, not surprised when he grasped her wrist.

"There's no reason to rush, is there? I can think of more fun things we can do this morning."

The tenor in his deep voice rumbled through her in the sexiest way and it was so hard not to slide back beneath the sheets along with him.

"I would… but I can't." She knew she had to give him something akin to the truth. "My life is way more complicated than you know and it's just better if I go," she said, pushing herself to her feet, aware of her nudity.

"Okay."

Okay? She spun around and wished she hadn't. He sat back, arms crossed over his broad chest, completely masculine and sexy. And he watched her, a barely-there smirk on his handsome face.

"Change your mind?" he asked.

She shook her head and rushed to dress in her gown from last night before she did as he'd asked and joined him in bed.

Chapter Four

FOR REMY, THE only thing harder than letting Raven leave without an argument was agreeing to keep things light and not serious between them. Because his mother raised him to be a gentleman—before he'd lost her, that is—he'd insisted on driving Raven home after she'd gotten dressed.

A detective at heart, he spent Sunday thinking about what made her tick. She kept to herself. Though she'd arrived at the wedding with Stevie, Raven normally kept her distance from people at work unless she was acting in her capacity as manager. Although she was friendly and polite, she was more solitary than not. Stevie was pushy, however, and she'd managed to become Raven's friend. Or as much of one as Raven would allow.

The only person Raven seemed close to was her brother, Caleb. When he and his young son visited the restaurant, Raven's face would light up, and she always took a break to spend time with them. That told Remy she didn't isolate herself from her family but she did from outsiders. Remy being one of them, and he'd obviously gotten too close.

He was itching to use his contacts, dig into her background, and find out why she was so closed off, but he opted to respect her feelings instead. Which meant he had no choice but to accept that whatever her reasons, it wouldn't be fair of him to push her for more than their one night.

The thought didn't sit well with him and he'd spent a couple of hours at the gym near his apartment working out his frustration, along with his brother, Dex. A former football player for the Miami Thunder, Dex was also a connoisseur of women—in other words, a playboy—but he was smart, and he agreed with how Remy had chosen to handle the situation with Raven.

By the time Remy strode into the bar around eleven a.m. on Monday, he had himself under control and was ready to deal with Raven like his employee and nothing more. For now.

He walked past the front tables, noting the staff getting the area ready for the lunch crowd, nodding at those who met his gaze.

He reached the bar where Stevie smiled at him. "Hi, boss."

"Good weekend?" he asked.

She nodded. "I slept in on Sunday and I needed it. You?" she asked in a serious tone, telling him she had no idea what had happened between him and Raven.

Of course, she knew that Raven hadn't shared an Uber home with her as planned but that seemed all. Anything else would be speculation unless Raven chose to tell her she'd been with Remy.

"Same," he muttered, though he wished he'd spent the day with Raven in his arms.

As if he'd conjured her, Raven walked out of the office area and strode over to Stevie. "When you're finished out here, Russell needs some help in the storage room."

"Sure thing." Smiling, Stevie headed into the back rooms, leaving Raven and Remy alone.

"Morning," he said, setting the tone of not making things awkward.

"Hi," she said, clutching an iPad to her chest.

Their gazes locked. And in her eyes, he caught a flare of desire before she tamped down on any emotion. She'd perfected the blank look brilliantly.

"Good rest of the weekend?" he asked.

"Sunday was fine." She took the stool beside where he stood, lowering herself on to it and placing her iPad on the counter. "But it was no match for Saturday night." Her sexy lips stretched into a sassy, almost secretive smile and his heart skipped a beat.

He assumed she'd ignore what went down between them. Her acknowledgment confirmed what he already knew. Raven would always surprise him and he enjoyed the unexpected.

"You don't say?"

She didn't reply but the lift of her lips remained.

He pulled out the seat next to her and sat, leaning in close enough to inhale peachy scent, which got his blood boiling. "I'd much rather have spent Sunday in that hotel bed with you."

Her cheeks flushed an attractive shade of pink. He wanted nothing more than to run his nose along her neck and breathe her in but she'd never forgive him if he acted on that instinct at work.

"Everything quiet here?"

She nodded. "All set for the lunch crowd up front."

The bar itself didn't open until later.

"Raven, got a minute?" She jumped at the unexpected intrusion.

Remy glanced over his shoulder to see her brother standing behind her, hands in his trouser pockets, a serious look on his face.

"Caleb!" She stared at him in surprise. "I didn't expect you to come by today. Why aren't you at work?"

Her brother was a partner at a high-end real estate firm uptown.

"We need to talk," he said, his mood far more somber than when he normally visited Raven. "It's urgent."

Raven's creamy skin paled.

Remy's protective instincts rose, but as much as he wanted to stick around to see what would get her so upset, he knew it wasn't his place to intrude and he rose from his seat.

"Hey, Caleb." He extended his hand and her brother shook it.

Caleb nodded at him. "Remy."

He stepped aside. "Take my chair. I need to check things in the back, anyway."

"Appreciate it," the other man said in a curt tone.

Though Remy walked away, he'd be keeping his eye on Raven.

★   ★   ★

RAVEN'S BROTHER TOOK the seat Remy had abandoned and sat down beside her, placing a white paper bag with familiar writing down on the counter. "Look what I brought you," he said, in an obviously forced, cheerful tone.

Despite the unease settling in her stomach, she grabbed for the bakery bag, opened it, and inhaled powdered sugar goodness. "Mmm. At least let me take a few bites of a donut before you wreck me."

She had no doubt something was wrong or he

wouldn't have taken the long trip upstate to pick up her favorite bakery treat, nor would he be here in the middle of the day.

Caleb worked hard so he could be home for his five-year-old son, Owen, in the evenings and when they came to visit, it was usually for dinner.

"Dig in." Caleb remained silent as she pulled out her treat and took a much-needed taste. "Yum. Amelia hasn't lost her touch."

Caleb smiled. "She said to tell you hi and she misses you."

"I miss her too." But Raven wouldn't visit her old friend's bakery in Chappaqua and risk running into her mother in town. That was a confrontation Raven avoided at all costs.

She placed the donut back into the bag to eat later, wiped her face with a napkin she grabbed from the counter, and faced her brother. "Okay, I'm ready. Talk to me."

He put his hand on hers and squeezed tight. "I need you to stay calm, okay?"

Her heart skipped a beat. "You're scaring me. Just get it over with. It's about *him*, isn't it?"

Caleb nodded. "Lance's getting out of prison early. In about two weeks."

"What?" She blinked, stunned, and leaned on the counter for support. Early release was impossible. The bastard ought to serve every day of his too short sentence.

"Breathe," her brother demanded, moving his hand to her back and rubbing for comfort.

She pulled in much-needed air. "How? He wasn't due out for another year!" And Raven thought she'd have that time to prepare and decide what to do before he was paroled.

"Overcrowding and good behavior, apparently." Caleb shook his head in disbelief. "Good behavior." He snorted, a scowl marring his handsome face.

Caleb was so good, so kind. The complete opposite of his fraternal, not identical, twin brother who lacked morals and a conscience. They did not look alike.

If it weren't for Caleb and the way he'd protected her, Raven might have gone mad while growing up within her adoptive family. Her birth father had run out on her mother before she'd been born and when Raven was five, her only parent was killed, hit by a car as she crossed the street on her way to work. Raven had vague memories of a soft voice and light brown hair. That was all.

Cassandra and Reginald Kane adopted her soon after, a lucky thing for a five-year-old in foster care, where babies were usually the first choice. She was brought home to meet her new brothers and she'd latched onto Caleb who she'd adored on sight. But from early on, she knew Lance was different. Colder. Meaner. And the older she got, the more she realized something was missing behind his brown eyes. He had no soul.

She sniffed and pulled back her shoulders, determined not to let the bastard defeat her.

Her big brother wrapped an arm around her shoulder and pulled her into him. "I wish you could move in with me and Owen."

She shook her head, a lump in her throat. "We both know that's a terrible idea. I don't want to put you in the middle and besides, I will never put Owen at risk."

"But—"

She pulled away and held up a hand, cutting him off. "Before you say Lance wouldn't hurt your child, remember what he did to Emily. I won't risk someone I love ever again."

In an effort to escape him once before, she'd left home at the age of twenty-one and moved in with a friend in the city. Not only had Lance found her, he'd beaten and was about to rape her roommate while Raven wasn't home. She'd arrived in the middle of the assault, had taken a bat and swung, hitting him in the shoulder to get him off her beaten friend. Raven shuddered at the memory and swallowed back the urge to throw up.

"Okay, but you're safe, right?" Caleb's voice helped ground her to the present.

She nodded. "Nothing here is in my name. The apartment where I'm staying is owned by the bar and it's alarmed." She wrapped her arms around herself and rubbed her goose-bumped skin.

"And no more visits you haven't told me about?" He pinned her with a worried gaze.

"None since I moved upstairs. I promise. I would have let you know." After Lance had been convicted thanks to Raven's testimony, he'd obviously made friends inside because she'd get periodic visits from released inmates, telling her that her brother said *hello*. Lance's way of letting her know that wherever she went, he'd find her.

This final move had enabled her more freedom since the apartment was listed under a corporate name and her lease was with Zach, personally, not through a property manager or real estate firm. He didn't know what she was running from but he hadn't questioned her need for secrecy. If he'd dug into her background and knew her story, he'd never let on, and for that she was grateful. Which made her wonder... if Zach did know about her past, had he told Remy?

She shook her head, discounting either notion. Both Remy and Zach had protective streaks a mile wide for anyone in their world. Despite Raven's deliberate attempts to remain aloof—until Saturday night, anyway—they'd pulled her into their world. She knew their family and their friends.

Zach might have his hands full now with his wife and her teenage sister, but Remy kept an eye on Raven. If he had any sense that danger lurked in her background and her future, he'd have mentioned it by now.

"Hey. Where'd you go?" Caleb asked.

She refocused on her brother. "Sorry. Just thinking."

He looked at her with a combination of pity and worry in his gaze. She despised the former and understood the latter.

"I'll do my best to keep an ear out and make sure I press our mother for details on her *favorite* son," he muttered, his tone laced with disgust.

Raven pursed her lips at that. Cassandra Kane spoiled her psycho child, turning a blind eye to his sociopathic behavior and taking his side no matter how bad the incident. *Always*. Which was why Raven put distance between them. Her father, a weak but kind man, passed away from a heart attack seven years ago, before Lance had tried and failed to rape Raven. Her mother had believed Lance over Raven and she'd moved out almost immediately afterward.

If Caleb could get information from their mother about Lance's whereabouts and plans post-release, that would help.

"Thank you, big brother." She managed a smile but knew Caleb didn't buy her forced cheer.

"I love you, Raven. If you need anything, day or night, call me. I'll get someone to watch Owen and I'll be there immediately."

Standing, she wrapped her arms around him and gave him a hug. "Love you too. You're a good man, Caleb. Your ex-wife was a fool to let my two favorite boys go."

He chuckled but didn't reply. He rose to his feet. "Are you going to be okay?"

She drew in a deep breath. "Yes. Don't worry about me."

He shot her an exasperated, are-you-kidding look, just as Remy strode over, joining them. God, the man was sexy. It didn't matter if he wore a tuxedo as he had Saturday night or a pair of black jeans and a button-down shirt open at his throat, the man oozed magnetic charm.

"Leaving already?" he asked Caleb.

Her brother nodded. "I have to get back to the office."

Remy looked from Caleb to Raven, his eyes narrowing on her face. "Is everything okay?"

She nodded. "Why wouldn't it be?"

Caleb leaned over and hugged her again. "Tell him everything. I need to know there's someone here looking out for you," he whispered in her ear before rising to his full height once more.

He said goodbye to Remy and told Raven to call him later, then he strode out of the bar.

Once they were alone, Remy stared at her, his amber eyes crinkled in concern. "Want to talk about it?" he asked.

She swallowed hard. "Not really... but I should."

Because not only had her brother made a valid point, but she owed Remy, the owner of this business, the truth since once Lance was free, Raven would be a walking target. If after he heard her story he wanted her to leave and not put their business or customers at risk, she would understand. Not that she had any idea where she'd go.

"My office?" he asked, tipping his head in that direction.

"Not here and not right now." She needed the day to process the news of Lance's imminent release. And to figure out how to spill her hardest secrets she'd always kept hidden.

"Dinner tonight? My place?" he asked. "It'll be more private."

She pulled in a breath, ignoring the fact that under

any other circumstances going to Remy's apartment would definitely lead to more than just talking. Not tonight.

"Yes, that sounds good."

He smiled that sexy grin she always fought to resist. "We'll head over together around ten? Pamela is working the late shift," he said of the assistant manager.

"Okay." And now it was time for her to do her job. The one thing in her life that until now, had been solid and secure.

Chapter Five

REMY WATCHED RAVEN work the rest of the night, aware she had something extremely troubling on her mind. He'd seen her nearly crumble against her brother, his heart squeezing at her obvious pain.

The night dragged on and when he realized he was doing nothing but staring at Raven, he holed up in his office, going through the last case he and Zach had handled. A runaway teen they'd managed to rescue from her sleazy high school teacher, reunite her with her family, and send the SOB to jail where he belonged. They kept meticulous notes should the case go to trial and with Zach's wedding coming up, Remy had taken lead on this investigation, hence it was his job to wrap it up. It also kept his mind off Raven and the fact that if he'd dug into her background, he'd be one step ahead of whatever the issue might be.

But then he'd lose her trust. So he worked. Until his watch reminded him to stand and walk around. As he circled the office, he glanced at the time.

Now, he could focus on Raven.

★　　★　　★

RAVEN RELUCTANTLY LET Remy pull her away from work. She had no desire to talk about her brother or his imminent release from prison but she understood the necessity.

They grabbed an Uber to his apartment, located farther downtown in Chelsea. He was silent on the ride over and she appreciated the time to think and figure out how to explain her past.

As they exited the vehicle and walked to the entrance of the building, a doorman greeted Remy by name. Inside was a stunning lobby, complete with a large sitting area and a concierge desk with an attendant behind it.

Remy placed his hand on her back as they strode through the marble lobby to an elevator set away from the main bank. His touch burned through her lightweight work shirt but she couldn't bring herself to step away. He pressed PH and she wasn't surprised he probably owned the top floor or that the elevator opened directly into his apartment.

They stepped off the lift and the doors closed behind them. Her brother resided in a brownstone on the Lower East Side and her mother and sister resided in Chappaqua, so of course Raven knew of wealth, but she no longer lived it. After she'd testified against

Lance, her mother had taken away Raven's access to the trust fund she didn't want anyway.

She was self-supporting and proud of it but she didn't begrudge anyone their money, however they came by it. But she respected Remy's work ethic and understood he hadn't needed to buy into the bar or PI business; he chose to.

"This way." He gestured farther inside the apartment and she followed him in. "Take off your shoes and get comfortable," he said, toeing off his leather slip-ons she had no doubt cost a pretty penny.

She removed her black, sturdy sneakers that kept her as comfortable as possible while on her feet all day and sighed in relief.

"How does Chinese sound?" he asked.

Her stomach let out a growl of approval and her cheeks heated at the sound. "Chinese sounds perfect."

"Good because I ordered it before we left the bar and the doorman put it in the kitchen." He met her gaze and winked.

Her body reacted to his flirtation and she felt a definite kick of desire low in her belly. "What if I didn't like what you ordered?" she asked, curiosity getting the better of her as she followed him into the kitchen. The delicious smell of garlicky food beckoned.

"Then I'd have asked you what you *do* like and

we'd wait for delivery."

She rolled her eyes. The man liked to take control but in this case, she was glad for it.

She took in the glory of the ultra-modern kitchen with white cabinets and stainless-steel appliances, all top of the line, of course. She helped him bring the boxes of food—not into the adjoining dining room—but to the oversized living room with comfortable-looking furniture.

He instructed her to set them on the table in front of the taupe-colored sofa and wood-glossed table, then returned to the kitchen for glasses.

While he was gone, she opened the tops of the white cartons, careful not to spill the contents on his table, though clearly it wouldn't bother him since they were eating so casually.

"Wine, beer, soda or water?" he called out.

"Soda is fine, thanks." Though she'd love a stronger drink to get through this talk, she wanted to be sober and aware of what she told him.

He returned, putting two cans of soda on the table, and put the ice-filled glasses on coasters. Once again, he disappeared into the kitchen, returning with stoneware plates, forks, knives, and napkins.

"There. All set." He sat beside her on the comfy, sectional. His thigh grazed hers but he didn't shift or move away. Neither did she.

He picked up each entrée and asked her if she wanted some, filling her plate as she nodded, only passing on one dish.

"You don't like shrimp?" he asked.

She shrugged. "I love shrimp but it gives me a ridiculous stomachache."

"Noted," he said, as if he'd need the information for the future. Which made no sense to her.

Still, they ate in comfortable silence and again, she appreciated his sensitivity in letting her finish the delicious meal before pressing her for answers.

"That was so good," she said, placing her dish on the table and leaning against the back cushion.

"It was," he agreed. "It's my favorite restaurant."

She smiled. "Well, good choice and thank you."

"My pleasure." The words rolled off his tongue, causing her body to heat with awareness.

Knowing her response could only lead to trouble, she needed distance. "I'll just clean up." She began to stand but he put a hand on her thigh. "Stay here. I'll take care of the mess later."

"But—"

"No."

She sighed, knowing he wasn't going to relent. "Okay. I take it now that you fed me, you want to know what went on between me and Caleb earlier?" She pushed herself back, turning so now her knees brushed his thighs and she faced him.

"Actually, I thought we'd open our fortune cookies."

She blinked in surprise. This man never said or did what she expected. "I love fortune cookies," she murmured. "Caleb and I used to read ours to each other when we were kids." She recalled the happy memory with a smile. There weren't all that many.

She glanced up and caught Remy studying her with interest, making her feel like he saw too much.

He reached over, lifted the two wrapped cookies from the table, and held them in the palm of his hand. "Pick yours."

She chose one and they ripped open their clear cellophane. She broke her cookie and pulled out the white note.

"You read first," Remy said.

She flattened the paper in her lap. A quick glance had her wanting to groan but there was no way out of it. "The man or woman you desire feels the same about you."

He gave a low growl—of what, she wondered. Approval? Agreement? Either way, the sound rumbled from his chest and suddenly, the need she'd banked along with the memories of Remy deep inside her surfaced. "Who makes these things up?" she asked, shifting uncomfortably in her seat.

"Someone who believes in taking chances?" he asked, his gaze hot on hers.

"Read yours," she muttered, hoping it was a lot more generic.

He glanced down and laughed out loud. "A good way to keep healthy is to eat more Chinese food," he said, breaking the sexual tension that had been heavy around them.

She grinned at the quote, relieved their smoldering attraction had been put on the back burner. "Now can I clean up?"

"Nope." He shook his head. "Now we can talk."

THE MAN OR woman you desire feels the same about you. Raven's fortune cookie was spot-on, Remy thought. But that wasn't why he'd brought her here. Of course, he'd wanted to enjoy dinner with her but he'd also wanted to give her a chance to relax before he pressed her for information.

He watched her twist her hands in her lap and waited as she worked up the courage to talk. Whatever she had to tell him was going to be bad and he braced himself, warning himself not to react, to stay calm and give her support.

"Okay." She tucked a strand of hair behind her ear

and blew out a long breath. "I already told you my mom died when I was five and I have no idea who my father was." She rubbed her hands on her dark jeans. "I ended up in foster care and then a miracle happened, at least according to the child welfare agent." In truth, it was a miracle she remembered that time considering how young she'd been, but her memory had always been good.

"I'm sorry you lost your mom." He wanted to reach for her but she held herself at an emotional distance and he sensed his touch wouldn't be welcome.

"Thank you," she murmured.

"What happened at the Kanes'?" He couldn't figure it out. She seemed to have a close relationship with Caleb.

"Lance happened." She wrapped her arms around her waist. "Caleb has a twin brother. Fraternal. They don't look alike. And he's a sociopath."

"A sociopath," Remy repeated, wondering if she was possibly exaggerating her description.

"With everything that definition entails. Lack of empathy, no remorse, he delights in causing pain, and he's mean." She visibly shivered as she spoke. "And when he wants to get away with his behavior, he can be charming and manipulative. And worse, he's my mother's favorite child."

Remy, too, shuddered at the description, imagining Raven as a little girl growing up in that house without her mother on her side.

"But I had Caleb. He's everything good in this world. He looked out for me and protected me when he could."

Remy had a solid feeling about her brother and was glad to know his gut instinct still worked. But her words chilled him. "What do you mean, he protected you *when he could?*"

"Well, he couldn't be home all the time, right? Lance would scare me, steal my things, return them broken and deny he did it. As I got older, he'd say sexually suggestive things and even sent me dick pics from a burner phone." She rubbed her hands on her pants and he understood her nervous energy.

"Raven, that's—"

"Disgusting. I know. Of course, without his face in the pictures as proof, my mother insisted it was someone else. And my father... he was just weak and deferred to her. But Caleb always believed me."

"Jesus." Unable to help himself, he grasped her hand, pulling it onto his knee, careful to keep her a respectful distance from his own dick.

"There's more." She looked at him, her eyes watery with tears, and he nodded. "So much more. My birth name is Raven Walsh, but my legal name is

Caroline Kane. I changed my name back to Raven when I left the Kane home."

Remy nodded. "I'd wondered why you and Caleb didn't share the same last name."

She lifted her shoulders and sighed. "I have so many reasons but none of that matters right now. What does is what happened the summer before I started college."

He waited for her to continue.

"I thought I was alone in the house with my sister and when I came out of the shower, I realized I'd forgotten clothes. So I stepped into the hall, intending to rush to my room. Lance was there and he... grabbed me. I tried to pull away and he shook me hard. He pushed me against the wall and was about to rip off my towel when Cara rushed into the hall and screamed for him to stop."

Raven didn't look at him but she pulled her hand back and Remy released her without question. He needed to hold her but she needed distance.

He scrubbed a hand over his face, attempting to collect his anger and stuff it down deep. During his time on the force, he'd seen plenty of crime victims. In the last year of rescuing runaways or kidnapped girls, he'd found traumatized females who needed his strength. He'd handled it all. But Raven's story felt more personal and he wasn't sure how to help her.

"What happened?" he managed to ask.

"Lance told her we were just roughhousing." Her lips twisted in disgust. "I was so shaken up but I still pulled Cara into my room, locked the door, and she called Caleb."

"Not your mom or dad?"

She gave him a wry smile. "Says a lot, doesn't it? Even at twelve, Cara knew to call our brother first."

"I take it Caleb believed you and your mother didn't?"

Raven nodded. "She said Cara must have misunderstood what she saw."

Remy's hands curled into fists by his sides. "So you didn't press charges?"

"Oh, I did. Caleb took me to the police station but nothing came of it. Not enough evidence, they said. I have no doubt my mother used her influence to make it all go away. Instead of waiting for school to start in the fall, I left soon after. I moved in with my best friend, Emily Devlin, who lived in the city."

Given how close Remy's family was, he couldn't imagine living in the home she'd grown up in or the isolation or fear she must have felt.

"I need a glass of water before I tell you more," Raven said and pushed herself off the sofa.

Before he could offer to get her the drink himself, she'd walked away. He assumed she needed a break, so he gave her the time, waiting until she returned, two glasses in hand.

"I thought you might want one." She placed both glasses on the coasters. Hers was already half empty.

"Thank you."

She smiled but it didn't reach her eyes.

He sighed. "Your story. It gets worse?" he asked, sensing her continued tension.

"Oh, yes. Lance had this obsession with me that not even my leaving put a stop to. One night, I was late getting home from the library. I came home to find he'd kicked open the door and Emily was lying on the floor, beaten and bleeding, and Lance was standing over her body. Her dress was pulled up and he was about to rape her," Raven whispered.

"Jesus."

"I went crazy. I grabbed the bat we kept near the front door and hit him over and over. It didn't seem to have an effect on him. He just stood there and took it until he finally turned and ran." She began to shake harder and Remy couldn't stand it another second.

He reached out and pulled her into him, wrapping her in a loose embrace meant to comfort. "Shh. That's enough for now." He didn't want her tortured any further. "Let's take a break."

She shook her head. "No. I need to finish. Then I can stuff it all back in the box inside me where it belongs."

"However you need to do this."

She pulled herself upright and pushed away from him. "Lance was arrested and this time not even my mother's name could get him off because they found DNA evidence on Emily and we both testified." She blinked back tears, showing him once again how strong she was.

"Lance went to prison and he was supposed to be there for another year, but apparently he's getting out in two weeks. Something about overcrowding and good behavior. And I *know* he's not finished with me."

She went on to explain that her friend, Emily, had moved and asked that they not keep in touch. She didn't want the reminders and though it had hurt, Raven understood. She'd moved out of their apartment, too, but somehow Lance was able to keep finding her. Sending his inmate buddies who were released to send his regards.

Remy's fury built with every word she'd told him.

"It's been quiet since I found the job and apartment with Zach but it won't stay that way. He threatened me after the trial. He swore I'd pay. And once he's out, he will do everything in his power to make sure I do."

"Raven—"

"I promised Caleb I'd tell you everything because

he thinks you can keep me safe, but that's not why I came here tonight. I wanted to give you the opportunity to tell me to leave, to fire me or let me quit, so I don't bring trouble to your business or your patrons."

He blinked in surprise. Was she so used to being alone and let down that she really thought he'd cast her out and leave her vulnerable to her psychotic brother?

"You're not going anywhere," he said in a too gruff voice.

"But the last person who I was close to paid a high price. Too high." She stood and he didn't need to be a mind reader to know she planned to leave.

He rose, blocking her path.

"Now that you know everything, you need to let me go. It's safer for you, for everyone around me."

He let out a low growl. "You don't need to protect me. I'm not Emily and I'll be damned if I let you deal with that psychopath on your own."

Remy had already been worked up over her painful past. Nothing would happen to her in the future. Not on his watch.

Chapter Six

REMY'S WORDS REVERBERATED in Raven's head. *You don't need to protect me. I'm not Emily and I'll be damned if I let you deal with that psychopath on your own.*

She hadn't come here for sex but she couldn't deny the need to find an escape in his arms. She no longer wanted to think about Lance or the fact that her time for feeling safe was limited.

Knowing Remy had her back helped calm her nerves and she couldn't deny her relief as every muscle in her body relaxed at his insistence she stay.

He might live to regret his decision but for tonight, she took him at his word.

"Thank you," she said, her shoulders sagging with relief. She met his gaze, hoping she conveyed the appreciation she felt toward him but also the desire.

She wanted him. She *always* wanted him.

She just knew better than to think they could have more than short term. Life rarely graced her with her deepest desires. Not for long.

Gazing into his golden eyes, she reached up and touched his cheek with her hand. "You're amazing, Remy. And I don't know whether to hug you or kiss you."

His lips lifted in a sexy grin. "I can answer that one easily." He stepped closer, bracing his hands on her hips as he lowered his head toward hers. "Kiss me, Raven."

"Okay, but this isn't about gratitude. It's about need," she said, wanting him to know her feelings.

Then she rose onto her tiptoes and their lips met, desire exploding between them. He lifted her and she wrapped her legs around his waist, their mouths still fused as he walked them to his bedroom and deposited her on the ultra-high mattress.

He stood by the bed, staring down at her with heat in his eyes. "Strip for me," he said, his voice huskier than it had been all evening.

She unbuttoned her jeans and pulled them down her legs, then moved on to other pieces of clothing, bra and panties included. All the while, watching as he undressed at the same time, revealing muscles that could only be the result of regular workouts and an erection that had her sex pulsing with desire.

He opened his nightstand drawer and pulled out a condom, tossing the packet next to her on the bed. Before she could shift positions and get comfortable, he grasped her ankles and pulled her toward him.

"Eek!" She let out a surprised squeak that quickly turned to a moan when his large hands spread her legs wide. And when she glanced up and saw the hungry look in his eyes, she was more than ready for whatever came next.

"You have no idea how often I've dreamed of tasting you."

His fingers pressed into her skin so deeply she thought she'd have his marks on her. That thought turned her on even more.

Before she could think or reply, he dipped his head and his tongue slid through her folds. She moaned, arching her hips and giving him better access. He took it, diving in like a starving man aiming to prove his words. His tongue was as talented as the man was relentless.

With every swipe and lick of his skilled tongue, he took her higher. Warmth and a delicious sense of need took hold and she rocked her sex against his mouth. His hands gripped her hips hard and held on as he continued his assault. It didn't take long before she was soaring, waves of pleasure taking her up and over, her climax bigger than any she'd had before.

His licks gentled as she came down from the high. He lifted his head and she was still dazed. She felt him lift his head from her thighs and place a small kiss on her skin. When she finally opened her eyes, he'd knelt on the bed, condom already on, and positioned between her spread thighs.

Her gaze met his.

As if he'd been waiting for her awareness, he buried himself deep in her body, filling her like he was meant to be there. Every part of her in tune to him, from the buzzing in her ears to the tingling in her breasts, to the way her inner walls contracted around his large cock.

"Remy." His name came out on a harsh breath.

"No one else, sweetheart. Just me."

Oh, this man was smooth, she thought, unable to withhold a grin at his cockiness. "Show me what you've got, then."

Her words freed his restraint and he began to move, thrusting in and out, each drive into her harder than the last. She loved how he didn't hold back. Her body began to awaken after the last orgasm and she began the climb toward ecstasy once more.

"More," she insisted, curling her fingers into the skin on his shoulders. If she was going to have his marks, she intended to leave some of her own.

His golden-brown eyes blazed with desire and he complied. Soon they had a rhythm of their own. He fucked her hard and yet when she let herself look into his eyes and take in his expression, though taut, in that moment, he was completely hers.

And that scared her.

But when he slid a hand between them, gliding his

fingertip over her slick folds and settling the pad over her clit, she arched her back and began to soar.

"Oh God. Remy, I'm coming." She screamed then, barely aware of him releasing himself at the same time but somehow knowing they came together.

NO SOONER HAD Remy pulled out of Raven, gone to the bathroom to take care of the condom, and returned to clean her up, she'd fallen fast asleep. Remy wasn't normally a cuddler with the women in his past, but he liked having Raven's head on his chest, her body splayed half across his.

As he listened to her breathing, he would have liked to sleep too, but his mind whirred with the information she'd given him about her brother. That son of a bitch had tortured and tormented her for years as a child, then did the unspeakable as an adult. He'd failed with Raven but succeeded with her friend, leaving Raven with scars of guilt and trauma. Though Remy knew nothing about Lance Kane, he'd arrested men like him, and Remy was sure the bastard intended to finish what he'd started years ago.

Which meant Remy needed to dig into the man and be ahead of his next move. He carefully slid Raven's head onto the pillow and moved away, stilling as she moaned and shifted, as if aware he'd left her. Or so he'd like to think.

He now knew some of Raven's past but sensed there was even more she hadn't shared. They needed time and he intended to make sure she was alive and safe in order to figure out what could be between them.

He rose and pulled on a pair of sweats, then made his way to his office and turned on his computer. He'd been a tech geek in high school and met Zach at Columbia, where they'd bonded over coding and hacking. Zach had been looking for his high school girlfriend whose entire family had disappeared overnight, while Remy had been seeking a way to avoid thinking about his mother's death. Or how things could have been different had he been home the night she died.

Unfortunately, they'd been caught hacking into a federal database while looking for Zach's ex-girlfriend, and in exchange for no charges being filed, they'd been hired by the federal government to test systems and prevent other hackers from accomplishing what they nearly had.

The deal they made with the feds meant he was able to continue on his career path in law enforcement. Otherwise, he would have been kicked out of school and worse, served time. That career path was important to him because he'd hoped it would allow him to catch criminals like the dirtbag who'd blamed Remy's father for his stock market losses and killed his wife in retribution.

He blinked, realizing that while he'd been thinking about the past, his fingers had been flying over the keyboard, digging into information on Raven's brother. Though he'd normally pull Zach in on a deep dive like this, his friend was on his honeymoon with his new wife, and Remy wouldn't disturb him.

Instead, he sent a few emails to friends in the right places. Now he needed to wait. It didn't take long for his mail to ding and a reply to come through. He hadn't expected Sean Andrews, his friend in the FBI who'd recently helped out Hadley, to be awake but he'd gotten lucky.

Remy opened the email and stared at the battered and bruised photos of Emily Devlin, taken in the hospital as evidence against Lance.

One look at the pictures and Remy's protective instincts kicked into high gear. No way would this son of a bitch lay a finger on Raven. Not while he was around.

"Knock knock."

Raven's voice startled him but he immediately clicked out of the mail program and hit the off button, shutting the computer down.

"I'm sorry I passed out on you," she said in a sleep-roughened, husky voice.

He shook his head. "It's fine. I wore you out." He winked, enjoying the flush that rose to her cheeks. "I couldn't sleep so I caught up on some work."

He glanced at her, realizing she wore one of his T-shirts that hung to her knees and a rush of possessiveness washed over him. Her hair was tousled and fell around his shoulders in sexy disarray. It was all he could do not to grab her and take her on his desk.

Instructing himself to rein it back because Raven wouldn't welcome his proprietary act, he kept things light. "Are you hungry?"

She shook her head. "No. I should get home, though."

"Or you could stay." So much for keeping it light, he thought.

Her eyes opened wide. The wariness he'd been trying to avoid had returned.

"Remy," she said in a warning tone.

"Raven," he mimicked back.

She strode over to where he sat. He turned the large, leather-cushioned office chair to the side. Wrapping one arm around her waist, he pulled her onto his lap. "Ladies first. What's on your mind? Why would staying be so bad?"

"It wouldn't. Not if we set parameters." She pulled

her lush lower lip between her teeth and released it with a pop. "I was thinking, we're both adults, right?"

He raised an eyebrow. "I sure as hell hope so, considering what we recently did together."

She let out an unexpected chuckle. "You know what I mean. Anyway, since we obviously both want each other—"

Understatement of the year, he thought. "Yes?"

"Well, I agree, you're not Emily and you can take care of yourself… and me. And now that you know about Lance, you're not going to let me run."

Damn right. He tightened his arm around her waist.

"So I thought we could have an arrangement."

"Such as?"

"I've seen you in occasional relationships through the years… well, not relationships exactly, but you tend to have flings."

He winced because she had a point. Until Raven, he'd never considered something serious.

"So I figured, we could be… you know, friends with benefits. At the bar, you're my boss, and there are boundaries, but other times when we're alone… we'd have the benefits. Would that be good for you?"

Fuck no, he thought. He wanted so much more. But that was the caveman in him talking. The rational, understanding human inside him knew he couldn't have all of Raven without slowly winning her trust. Which meant giving her what she needed. Time. Space.

He placed his finger on her moist lower lip, running the pad over her flesh. "If that works for you, it does for me," he said in a gruff voice.

Her shoulders sagged in what must have been relief and his heart squeezed as he realized what it must take for her to hold herself together. She was wound so tight and pressed down so much fear. Something had to give. He wanted to be her safe place.

"So we're good?" she asked.

Meanwhile, as she sighed and wriggled on his lap, his dick grew hard and he gritted his teeth against the desire he wouldn't be acting on.

"We're good," he assured her.

She hugged him, placing her head on his shoulder and her chest against his, as she breathed against his neck. "Thank you, Remy. I feel safe with you."

And those words both solidified his decision to go slow and caused a warm feeling in his chest, and his heart beat in time with hers.

When she decided to go home anyway, he understood, and let her go.

Chapter Seven

S TERLING FAMILY GATHERINGS were large and loud, and where they were located was decided on the spur of the moment. That was Remy's family. No planning, just an agreement to get together. Sometimes it was to catch up because it had been a while and others it was to celebrate.

Today was the latter. Aiden, their traveling journalist brother, had come home from the dangerous war zones he reported from. Whether it was for good or not was anyone's guess. In all probability, Aiden wasn't sure either.

Where Remy dove into the police force and now dealt in missing people to assuage his guilt over not being home when their mother was killed, Aiden ran away from his regret for being asleep upstairs during the murder. It didn't matter that logic dictated neither were to blame. Self-recrimination was hard to let go of.

Remy's family sat around a long table. The gathering included their father, Alex, and housekeeper, Elizabeth Snyder, though they called her Lizzie. She was an attractive woman, slightly younger than his dad.

Lizzie came with the house when Alex had purchased the property in Old Brookville. A widow, she resided in the gatehouse on the property when the original residents owned the place and her staying was part of the sales agreement.

Her daughter, Brooklyn, grew up in the gatehouse and was best friends with his sister, Fallon. The women couldn't be more different. Fallon was a Bohemian artist and owned a gallery. Brooklyn was a corporate type who dressed much more formally. Since graduating, she'd worked at the Sterling family business with Jared, who was the CFO under their dad. But the women couldn't be closer.

The rest of his siblings were already seated too, as they waited for Aiden. While the joking and laughter went on around him, Remy kept an eye and ear on Raven, who sat with a laptop behind the bar. Whether she was absorbed in bar business or avoiding catching his gaze, he didn't know.

"She won't disappear if you take your eyes off of her, you know," Dex said.

Remy glared at his brother. "It's not like you'd know what it was like to settle on one woman," he muttered.

Dex chuckled, not the least bit insulted. He loved his bachelor lifestyle in a way Remy never had, especially after being married. Once he and Sadie had divorced because she couldn't live with his *dangerous* job as a detective, being alone in the large house felt... odd.

Sadie hadn't wanted anything from him except a small lump sum to get back on her feet, leaving Remy with the house he'd bought, which he sold almost immediately after their separation. Getting back into the dating game sucked. He didn't like it the way Dex did but Remy had his share of women.

Maybe it Dex's years of playing star quarterback and being idolized by women all over the state of Florida. Who knew?

"Is Raven okay?" Dex asked more seriously. "She's a little pale."

Remy sighed. "Not really."

Raven's truths were her own but even Remy needed to let someone know what was going on. "Look, this has to stay between us, but she has a psychotic brother who is getting out of prison and he's going to target her."

Remy went on to explain her past to Dex. All of it, from adoption on. "Though I have a feeling there's more I don't know."

Dex ran a hand through his hair, messing up the top in a way no style could capture. He dabbled in modeling, and had done some ads in the past. "What you told me is enough."

"I figured you'd understand her considering you were also adopted."

"Except I got the good family and a chance to heal." Dex lifted his gaze to where Raven was still working behind the bar. "Her, not so much."

Remy nodded. "Exactly. I'm trying to show her she can trust me but it's a long, rough road. Right now she thinks we're friends with benefits." He let out a snort. "As if I'd settle for that."

Dex didn't smile. "Just be careful you aren't falling back into old habits."

"Meaning?"

"Never mind," Dex muttered. "If I need to bring it up again I will."

Remy frowned but decided to ignore his sibling. He wasn't ready to go down that road, even if he knew what his brother was getting at.

"I know you'll make sure Raven is protected and you'll be there when she finally gives in to your charm."

"Always helpful." Remy slapped Dex on the back.

He and Remy were the same age which had also helped when Dex's parents died, courtesy of a drunk driver. Witnesses said the couple had been arguing at the time, which contributed to his dad not being able to swerve to avoid the other vehicle in time.

Dex had always been the next-door neighbor who

hung out with the Sterling kids to avoid the constant yelling in his own home. After his parents passed away, Alex and his mom, Gloria, had given him a home and later, when Dex was ready, had adopted him.

"Any ideas what you're going to do now that you've retired from football?" Remy picked up a glass of water and took a long sip.

Dex shook his head. "Ian's trying to convince me to take a job in the front office but I've got no interest in that kind of desk job."

Ian Dare, the team owner, wanted Dex to take a desk job? That wouldn't be happening, Remy thought. "What about broadcasting?"

Between his brother's good looks, talent on the field, and inherent smarts, something a quarterback needed to succeed, Dex would make a phenomenal sportscaster.

He leaned back and grinned. "Let's just say my agent has many irons in the fire."

His agent was Austin Prescott, one of the best in the business. "I have no doubt you'll be signing a multimillion-dollar deal soon."

"Maybe. There's a lot to consider."

Just then, Remy caught sight of Aiden walking into the bar and rose from his chair. "Look who's here! The wanderer has returned."

His words got the rest of the family's attention and soon their world-traveling brother was being embraced by the family, one by one.

After a hug and slap on the back by Dex, Remy grabbed his middle sibling's forearms. "You look good," he lied.

Aiden had dark circles under his eyes and the weight of the world on his shoulders. But there was time for one of the siblings to crack his hardened shell.

"Home to stay?" Dex asked, as Remy's throat filled at the possibility Aiden might take off again.

"I'll decide for sure after my vacation time's up. Right now, I just want to enjoy being home."

In other words, don't pressure him. "Got it," Remy said. "Take a seat and let's do just that."

As Aiden pulled off his jacket and hung it over the empty chair, Remy's gaze came to rest on Raven's once more. A wistful look was on her face, her eyes sad, lips pursed as she watched his family. She stared at Brooklyn, who'd come around to talk to Aiden, then Raven's gaze slid to his father and Lizzy, whose heads were tilted toward each other.

Suddenly she put the iPad onto the counter, pushed up from her chair, and walked out from behind the bar and toward the kitchen.

Without hesitation or a word to anyone, Remy shoved back his seat and headed to find her.

★　★　★

RAVEN NEVER CONSIDERED herself a jealous or envious person and she couldn't say those were the emotions squeezing inside her chest now. But watching Remy's big family caused a pang of sadness to fill her at what might have been if her father hadn't run off, if her biological mother hadn't passed away, if she hadn't been adopted. If the Kanes had been a normal family.

She jerked her head from the warm, fuzzy scene, placed her iPad on the counter and strode to the kitchen, certain she could find something to do to keep herself busy. The last thing she wanted to be was the outsider looking in.

Once in the professional kitchen, she said hello to the chef and his staff. Noticing an empty counter that needed wiping down, she picked up a rag and began to clean.

She'd just finished and tossed the dishrag into a gray bin when the double doors swung open and Remy walked inside, coming straight toward her. He looked sexy, as usual, wearing a pair of dark jeans and sneakers, and a men's white dress shirt, rolled at the sleeves and unbuttoned at the neck. The urge to place her nose into that space and sniff his bare skin was strong.

"Hiding out?" he asked, obviously oblivious to her sudden need to lose herself in him.

She forced a smile. "I figured it was time to check on Thomas."

"You lie, little bird," the chef said, using his nickname for her based on her name. "I never need checking up on."

She shrugged. "What can I say? I wanted a few minutes away from the crowd."

Remy glanced at the chef, who'd returned to chopping chicken for the tenders they served before giving her his full attention. "Everything okay?"

She nodded then, with a tip of her head, led him out of the kitchen and into the hall. If she was going to be honest, she wanted privacy. It also wasn't like Raven to open a vein for anyone, male or female. But, as she was coming to realize, Remy wasn't just anyone.

She leaned against the wall behind her and drew a deep breath. "I was watching all you Sterlings and it got me thinking about how different my life would have been if the people who adopted me had been more like your family. Warm, caring, supportive." Her chest tightened at the hurt she still felt when she allowed herself to think too hard.

"Nobody's family is perfect," he said, reaching out and curling a strand of hair that had escaped her ponytail around his finger. "In public, you only see a snippet of life."

"I suppose."

He placed his palm against the plaster over her shoulder. "I have no idea how much you know about my life but it wasn't all sunshine and roses."

She really had no idea what his childhood had been like, and met his gaze, curious about what he had to say.

"When I was seventeen, my mother was murdered by a financial client of my father's."

She gasped, covering her mouth, before dropping her arm once more. "I'm so sorry. I had no idea." And she hated that she'd inadvertently caused him to bring up his pain.

"I'd like to say it was a long time ago, and I'm over it but... it stays with me." He swallowed hard, his Adam's apple bobbing. "Aiden was home sleeping, Dad was at a business dinner, and the rest of my brothers and my sister were busy out of the house, too. At different places. It doesn't matter. Mom and I were supposed to go out for dinner but when a girl I'd been into broke up with her long-term boyfriend and showed me some attention..."

"You went for it," Raven said with an understanding smile.

He raised one shoulder and lowered it again, trying to seem casual, but his pain was somehow hers. She felt the heavy, rhythmic beating of her heart, the fullness in her throat, and knew he was experiencing the same emotions.

"I was a typical teenager," he said with disgust. "Selfish and self-absorbed. Mom said she understood and told me to go. If I'd just gone out with her like we'd planned…"

Raven clasped his free hand. "Then maybe you'd have been hurt or killed, too. Or maybe it was fate and the murderer would have found another time when your mom was alone. All I know is you can't blame yourself."

He curled his fingers around her hand, squeezing to express his gratitude. "As a kid, I couldn't get past it. Now, as an adult, I *know* all the same things you just said but it's hard not to blame myself."

"I know," she whispered, her gaze on his.

"But we're both doing the same thing. There's no point in wishing away something bad. You can't change what happened with the Kanes any more than I can with my mom."

She nodded and tipped her head up, her eyes locking on the warmth in his golden-brown gaze. Leaning down, he brushed his lips over hers. Once, twice, then a third time that made her moan and press her body against his.

"Raven Walsh, stop making out and get your ass

out here. The cake from Juniper's is here and as manager, you need to sign for the order," a familiar voice called out.

Stevie.

Like caught teenagers, she and Remy jumped back, Raven mortified she'd crossed boundaries at work.

"Get that look off your face," he whispered. "You did nothing wrong. Stevie's your friend. It's all good."

A friend she needed to keep at a distance once her brother got out of prison. She shook her head and pushed that thought aside. She still had time.

"She's lucky I like her or I'd fire her," Remy muttered.

But they both knew he'd never do such a thing. Stevie was the best of the waitstaff they had.

"Boss, your family's waiting," Stevie called, this time in a singsong voice.

He shook his head, a smirk on those perfect lips.

"We'll pick this up again later," he said in a gruff voice.

"So sure of yourself, aren't you?" she teased, surprising herself again.

She liked this lighter side she rarely showed. Too bad it'd be locked down soon enough. Not wanting to deal with thoughts of Lance, she pushed the reality aside.

"After I finish with my family, I need to meet with

a client," Remy was saying and she focused on his steady voice instead. "Can I come by afterward?"

Leaning down, she expected another slide of his mouth over hers. Instead, he licked her bottom lip and she groaned.

"Vanilla and mint. Yum," he said, then stood to his full height.

She glanced down and realized his cock was thick and aroused, tenting against his jeans.

He gave her a soft, pleading stare. "Please?"

She laughed at his antics. "Yes! Now go before someone comes looking for you again."

Obviously satisfied he'd gotten his way, he winked, and walked away, giving her the perfect view of a perfect ass.

THE BAR GOT busier after the Sterling family left and Raven even helped serve drinks. By the time the night ended, she was tired and ready to turn in for the night. Stevie walked out to an Uber she'd called and waved good night. Raven locked up the restaurant.

She strode past the tables and chairs to the door in the back that led to the apartment she rented. Stepping out, she locked up and set the alarm to the bar. One of the things she liked about the setup was that she had to go through the business in order to reach her front door. Nobody could sneak in and she felt safe.

At her apartment door, she unlocked the Medeco lock on the bottom and the deadbolt on top. Once inside, she unset the alarm and locked up behind her, resetting the alarm.

"Whew." She kicked off her shoes, leaving them by the door. All she wanted was a hot shower and to crawl under the covers and get some sleep.

The apartment had come decorated in furniture much nicer than anything she'd be able to afford on her own. She had a feeling Zach had initially liked her enough or sensed she was one of his needy women and cut her a break on the rent. Either way, the place was homey and perfect for her.

She entered her bedroom. Just as she reached for the light switch, the window by her bed shattered. She screamed and out of instinct, rushed out and slammed the door behind her.

Though she hoped the blare of the alarm had scared them off, she ran out of the apartment and rushed back to the bar, locking herself inside.

Chapter Eight

REMY DROVE HOME from his surveillance mission. He'd caught a man playing basketball with his son while suing his employer because he'd slipped on a wet floor that hadn't been marked with cones or signs. Once Remy forwarded the photographs to his client, their business would use them during the ongoing trial, no doubt ending things then and there.

Remy hated cases of insurance fraud. People using fake injuries to defraud the companies for cash disgusted him, not just because it was wrong but every time they succeeded, they made it harder for those truly hurt to be compensated the amount they deserved. Missing people satisfied something in Remy's soul but when those jobs were scarce, which was a good thing, he and Zach often helped companies prove illegitimate claims.

It wasn't that either he or Zach needed the money. They each came from wealthy families and their college hacking venture had led to them meeting important contacts, one of whom had purchased the anti-hacking software they'd developed, paying a huge amount of money.

As a result, both Zach and Remy were wealthy in their own right but they weren't lazy and liked to work. Admittedly, Remy enjoyed the job more when he didn't have a willing woman waiting for him but he was on his way to Raven's now.

He was drumming his fingers against the steering wheel in time to the beat of the music on the radio when his cell phone rang and the name of the alarm monitoring company showed on the dashboard screen. The clock nearby said it was nearly eleven.

Remy answered via Bluetooth speaker. "Remy Sterling here." The bar occasionally had alarm faults and he was used to these calls.

"Mr. Sterling, this is Paul with Alpha Monitoring. What is your security code?"

The company was required to hear the code in order to know they were relaying information to the right person.

"Gloria," he said, a pang twisting his stomach as he spoke his mother's name. Once he'd taken over the New York City bar, it had made sense for him to change the code to something he'd easily remember.

"Thank you. The alarm at The Back Door was triggered. Zone 24, far back apartment window, glass break. The police have been dispatched."

Remy had made it his business to know the zones in case of an emergency and this was Raven's apartment, her bedroom window.

"Thanks," he muttered and disconnected the call. Ignoring his increased heart rate and the panic that spread through him, he pressed his foot on the accelerator, instructing his vehicle to call Raven's cell phone.

It went straight to voicemail and the ride from Cliffside Park, New Jersey, to Manhattan felt twice as long. Remy drove well over the speed limit, his pulse hammering in his throat the entire way.

As far as he knew, Lance was still behind bars, and Remy hung on to that thought, pushing aside his assault on Emily and his attempt on Raven. By the time he finally pulled up to the back parking lot, parked and rushed to the bar door, his nerves were shot. He was glad the main entrance was in the rear, hence the name of the bar, so he didn't have to waste time going around to the front of the building after parking.

A uniformed cop stood at the patron entrance. Remy flashed his license and explained he owned the place and was close friends with the tenant.

"Remy?" Raven's voice called out to him and the officer stepped aside.

He took three steps and Raven came running, crashing into him and wrapping herself around him like a spider monkey.

Carly Phillips

"I've got you," he murmured, as he held on to her, giving her the time she needed to calm down. Time he needed as well.

Raven held on to him, breathing hard into his neck.

"Ma'am?" The voice came from farther inside the bar.

Raven released her hold and turned, but Remy wasn't ready to let go and pulled her against him, so they faced the second officer together.

"Yes?" she asked.

Despite Remy's desire to take over, he knew Raven needed control so he kept her tucked against him, taking what he needed, too.

"The apartment is clear," the uniformed man said. "Nobody was inside but the window is shattered. It's unlikely anyone could have crawled through the glass without being cut up and leaving a trace of blood. But we still need you to look around and see if anything is missing."

She stiffened against Remy.

"Come on. I'll go with you," he said.

She drew a deep breath and he watched from the corner of his eye as she paused. He had no doubt she was mentally arguing with herself until she nodded, straightened her shoulders, and stepped out of his embrace. On her own, like the brave woman he knew her to be, she walked toward the back of the bar. She might be shaking inside but she'd pulled herself together and while he was glad, he knew that meant she no longer needed him. Nor would she show any further weakness.

Once in the hall outside her open door, she stepped inside and looked around, then made her way toward the bed.

"Look, don't touch. We don't want to mess with anything forensics might discover," the officer said.

Remy did his best not to roll his eyes. Of course, they would find Raven's fingerprints all over her own apartment but he let the officer maintain his jurisdiction over the scene.

Raven took in her bedroom and the destruction near her bed. "My jewelry is still on the dresser, my laptop is on the nightstand that isn't near the window." She paused, still glancing around. "My Kindle is on the bed…" She shook her head. "Nothing seems missing… Oh my God."

He glanced over to see she'd lost all color in her cheeks. "Raven?"

She walked stiffly to the window, stopping near the broken glass on the floor. Coming up beside her, Remy placed a hand on her shoulder, and she flinched.

"Sorry," she muttered. "You startled me."

"What's wrong?" he asked.

The police officer stood off to one side, his gaze narrowed, watching them intently.

She pointed toward the shattered glass with items laying among the shards. "That broken piece. It's a collectible Caleb got me for my birthday. I think I was around fifteen. He gave me a Daenerys Targaryen Funko Pop. You know, from *Game of Thrones*. I loved the show and that present set a precedent for each birthday after. It was our special thing. Whatever I was into, Caleb managed to find a matching gift."

"Who's Caleb?" the cop asked, his phone out, finger hovering to type important notes.

Remy glared at him. "Her brother, Caleb Kane. Now let her get through this her way."

"Officer Jones." A familiar man in a sport jacket walked in and snapped at the younger cop who immediately clenched his jaw but straightened his shoulders. "I'll take over."

Remy breathed out a sigh of relief. "Detective Garrett Lewis. How are you?"

His old friend on the force shook his hand. "I heard your name over the police radio. I was in the neighborhood, so here I am."

Remy was grateful. "Garrett, this is Raven Walsh. She's renting the unit. Raven, this is an old friend of mine. Detective Lewis."

Garrett treated Raven to an understanding smile

that never failed to calm a victim.

"Hi, Detective." She swallowed hard.

"Seems like you were explaining something when I walked in. Why don't you go on?"

Remy put a hand on her lower back, keeping his touch light, to encourage her.

She nodded. "I was saying, my brother bought me that broken collectible." She gestured to the blonde doll-like figure lying amid the glass. She tucked a strand of hair that had fallen from her ponytail behind her ear. "He also bought me the matching collection of Edgar Allan Poe Funko Pops when I got older and more into dark stories, and look." She pointed to her nightstand, also covered with glass. "Poe's head is broken off his body."

"Shattering glass wouldn't have done that damage," Garrett muttered.

"Lance, on the other hand, would. And he has." She spoke with deliberate precision, clearly forcing herself to keep it together and not show her panic.

"What do you mean, he *has*?" Garrett asked.

She rubbed both her arms with her hands. "He did the same thing to my first Funko. He broke Daenerys' head and put it in my bed. He'd just seen *The Godfather*."

Garrett met Remy's gaze and he knew, without words, what his friend was thinking. No sane man would replicate the horse's head scene in *The Godfather.*

"Caleb replaced the doll but the damage was done… at least in my mind. Lance liked to terrorize me."

While Remy grasped both her cold hands in his, Garrett asked, "Who is Lance?"

"Her other brother. He's Caleb's twin and he's a sociopath. He's been doing time for attempted rape and assault but she got word from her brother he was getting out early."

"I thought I had time before they let him out," she said.

"Normally, the department of corrections calls the victim and gives them a heads-up," Garrett said. "As long as they've registered their information with the state."

She nodded. "But I wasn't the victim, my roommate was. I was the star witness." She spun to face him. "Emily! Someone needs to make sure she knows about Lance."

"Maybe someone already did." Garrett made notes in his cell phone. "Look, I need to find out if Lance has been released before we can question him."

Remy set his jaw then spoke. "If he hasn't been let out yet, then he sent one of his minions." He explained to Garrett how Lance had kept an eye on Raven until she'd moved here.

"We'll make sure she's okay," Garrett promised.

A knock sounded on the bedroom door. "Forensics," a redheaded woman said, walking inside the room with her bag and kit.

"We need to let her do her job. Raven, do you have some place to stay?" Garrett asked.

"She's staying with me," Remy said in a definitive tone that brooked no argument. If Raven wanted to fight him, she'd discover his stubborn side. When it came to her safety, he wouldn't give in.

REMY LED HER outside the bedroom of horrors that she'd never be comfortable in again. Once in her family room, she could catch her breath. Actually, she'd begun to breathe the minute she'd heard Remy's voice.

She looked around the apartment like she'd never seen the place before.

"We're leaving town," Remy said.

She blinked, startled out of her thoughts. "What? No."

Her words surprised her. For years, she'd told herself when Lance was released, she'd run, so she was shocked to discover, at the mention of doing just that, her spine straightened and she shook her head.

"You want to stay?" he asked, surprised.

She raised her chin. "This is my life and I'm going to fight for it."

A slow smile lifted his lips, his eyes warm as he met her gaze. "Okay. Then at least come stay with me so we know you're safe. Let's see how things play out."

Instinct would have had her saying no, she could handle herself, but Raven had read too many books where the heroine was, as readers liked to call it, too stupid to live. She might be wary of getting too close to Remy but she'd be a fool to fight him when it was in her best interest to go somewhere safe.

"Okay. After how easily Lance broke in and touched my things, I doubt I'll feel safe staying there alone again. So yes, until I can figure out my next steps, I'll go with you," she said.

His wide smile told her he thought he'd won a huge victory. She shook her head and didn't reply.

"Forensics won't let you back in while they're working. I'll just have Fallon drop off some clothes for you in the morning."

It was a testament to how freaked out she was that she didn't argue with him.

A little while later, once the police took her cell phone number and found out where she'd be staying, she and Remy finally walked into his apartment. The place was familiar since she'd eaten dinner with him and done oh so much more.

He stopped short in the hallway leading to his room. "For tonight you can borrow a T-shirt from me. I've already texted Fallon and she said she would drop off clothes and toiletries in the morning."

"I hate to put her out," Raven said, the idea of being an imposition finally dawning on her.

"Fallon is happy to help." He gestured to his bedroom and said, "Ladies first."

She didn't know what to expect but that hadn't been it. "Remy, I'm not sure me sleeping in your room is a good idea."

He leaned a shoulder against the doorframe and faced her. After a full day, he had sexy facial scruff and his eyes were heavy-lidded. "Are you still upset? Scared or worried?" he asked.

She released the lower lip she hadn't realized she'd pulled between her teeth. "Yes."

"And are we still *friends with benefits*?" He raised his eyebrows, the question clearly important to him.

She nodded.

"And friends help friends out. You don't need to be alone tonight, or any night you're here. Won't you feel safer with me?"

She sighed. "Of course. But—"

"But nothing. Tonight, all I want to do is hold you

so you can relax. Got any objection to that?" he asked.

"Of course not." How could she say otherwise? "But, Remy?"

"Yes, Raven?" His lips lifted in a knowing smirk.

She rolled her eyes at his mocking attitude. "Just because we're sharing a room, a bed, and after tonight, probably having sex—"

"Definitely having sex."

She shook her head at his bold claim. "Fine, definitely having sex, that doesn't mean anything's changed. We're still *not* in a relationship."

Ignoring the slight twitch in his eye wasn't easy. She didn't want to hurt him. She just needed to hang on to that piece of independence she might need if Lance decided to go after anyone else she cared about. Because in that case, she'd be out of here without looking back, and she couldn't let herself get emotionally attached, she thought, ignoring the little voice that told her she already had.

Chapter Nine

REMY WAS RIGHT. Sleeping in his bed, wrapped in his arms, inhaling his warm, musky scent... Raven had slept better than she had in years. Probably since the night Emily had been attacked and Raven had decided it was time to live alone.

Stretching her arms above her head, she yawned and decided to take a hot shower. Remy wasn't beside her and she assumed he was either working in his office or in the kitchen drinking his morning coffee.

She slid out of bed and discovered he'd left another one of his T-shirts hanging over a brown, leather club chair in the corner. On the table beside it was a hardcover novel. She stepped over, saw the Steve Berry title, and smiled. Remy obviously liked thrillers. It wasn't hard to picture him stretched out, feet up in the chair, reading as a way to relax before bed.

Nor could she deny she liked learning personal things about the man she was falling for despite her better judgment. How could she not appreciate his protectiveness, understanding, and yes, his often demanding ways? Ways that were going to rear their ugly head when she told him she wanted to go out tonight. But she'd meant it when she said she wasn't going to let fear rule her life.

Knowing she had some time, she looked around and found a pad and paper, pleased she didn't have to use her phone's notebook app. She did her best thinking when she handwrote her poetry. Poetry nobody knew she wrote. As she sat by the window in his recliner, the words came to her and she knew *this* was what she'd be reading tonight. Something lighter than she'd thought of before. Because there were moments… with Remy… when she felt like a different Raven.

With a sigh, she grabbed his shirt and headed into the luxurious bathroom. Last night she'd rinsed her only pair of panties and hung them to dry, sleeping without them. It hadn't been easy to lay enveloped in Remy and ignore the desire racing through her veins. But he'd been right in saying she needed to relax and feel safe. Faster than she could have imagined, and definitely quicker than if she were alone, she'd fallen asleep.

She took a quick shower, using all the jets in the glass enclosure, enjoying the pulsing as each hit her muscles. Closing her eyes, she appreciated the massage-like feel. After washing her hair with Remy's shampoo and using his soap, she rinsed, shut the water and stepped out onto a soft, comfortable mat.

As she dried herself off, she couldn't help but notice she smelled like Remy. And she liked it. She pulled on his shirt that came to right above her knees, and tied up her hair in a messy, wet bun.

Before joining Remy, she noticed her cell phone on the dresser, the only personal item she'd taken with her other than the clothes she'd worn yesterday.

Picking it up, she called Caleb and relayed last night's events. "So I'm staying at Remy's," she told him, knowing he'd flip out if he couldn't find her.

"Why didn't you call me? I'd have come right over."

She smiled at his expected answer. "Because you have Owen and you'd have had to find a sitter and Remy showed up soon after. I'm safe here."

Her brother let out a rough breath. "Mom didn't mention Lance was out early."

And Raven hadn't heard from Emily, not that she'd expected to. She hoped her old friend was okay and made a mental note to ask Remy to follow up with Garrett and find out what he could about her.

Caleb groaned. "I know you're right but I don't like that I can't be with you. Did you call Cara?"

Raven closed her eyes for a brief moment. "No. I'm so frazzled I forgot. Would you mind doing it? Tell her I'll get in touch when I'm more settled."

Her younger sister was the baby her mother had in

the hopes she'd have a *dutiful* daughter—unlike Raven—as she'd been informed so many times. Luckily, maybe because she was blood-related, Lance had left Cara alone… so far.

But Cara wasn't the agreeable child Cassandra had wanted, and she'd recently moved out of their mother's home to attend college in the city. She lived in a doorman apartment with a roommate, also keeping her distance from their mother and her toxicity. Cassandra didn't like it but she had paid for Cara's apartment choice thanks to the safety features.

"I'm worried about you," Caleb said, breaking into her thoughts.

"If it's about my physical safety, I'm okay in Remy's penthouse apartment. Emotionally, I'm holding it together. That's all I can say."

Caleb groaned. "Owen, stop playing with the eggs and eat them," he said. "You're shaken up. I can tell."

"I'll be fine, Caleb. I won't let Lance win."

"I agree. Listen, I need to go help the little troublemaker with breakfast. Don't be insulted if I call Remy and I *will* check on you later. Love you," her brother said, then went on to explain to her adorable nephew why eggs belonged on plates and not the kitchen table, before disconnecting the call.

Still smiling, Raven made the large, king-sized bed, smoothing the wrinkles on the cocoa-colored comforter, and readjusting the pillows, taking her time to inhale Remy's arousing scent.

Then she walked out of the bedroom in bare feet and made her way to the kitchen. Voices sounded from the direction in which she was headed. Remy's she recognized. The female's she couldn't place, and a sudden pang of jealousy twisted low in Raven's stomach. Until she remembered him saying Fallon would be dropping off clothing this morning, and she chided herself for being silly.

Raven had met everyone in Remy's family over the last couple of years but she couldn't be sure it was Fallon's voice she heard. But for her to be jealous? No. That wasn't okay.

She and Remy weren't in any kind of committed... anything. Raven had clearly nixed the idea of a relationship. So even if it wasn't Fallon, Raven told herself to suck it up and she strode into the kitchen.

"Good morning," she said, cringing at the overly cheery sound of her voice.

"Raven, come on in." Remy held out an arm and fool that she was, she walked right into the crook of his shoulder. "You remember my sister Fallon, right?"

"Of course," Raven said, with a genuine smile. Because Fallon wasn't one of Remy's women. God, she was being ridiculous.

The familiar-looking female in front of her had

distinctive Sterling features, including golden-brown eyes similar to Remy's. Unlike most of their male siblings who dressed in suits or expensive slacks and button-down shirts, Fallon's taste could only be described as boho. Unconventional skirts, bright colors, layered tops and vests, she was the most casual Sterling and her bright grin said she was happy to see Raven.

Without hesitation, Fallon stepped forward and pulled Raven into a hug. Raven wasn't used to others touching her, especially the women in her life she tried to keep at a distance, but Fallon's hug felt good.

"I'm so sorry about what's going on with your brother," Fallon said.

Remy cleared his throat as if reminding his sister she'd crossed a line mentioning Lance.

She winced and went on. "Anyway, I brought you two of my skirts and tops, a pair of ballet slippers, I hope you fit into an eight, and I stopped by a department store and picked up some personal items and makeup." She shrugged. "I did my best."

"You're the best, Fallon. Really. I appreciate it so much. Let me know what I owe you," Raven said.

The other woman waved a hand, dismissing the notion. "Don't worry. Remy already paid me back."

Of course he had, which meant he wouldn't take her money, not that Raven wouldn't try to reimburse him.

"I've got to get going," Fallon said. "Raven, if you need anything, just give me a call. Remy has my number." She smiled at her, then walked over and kissed her brother on the cheek. "Bye. Be good."

Her laugh followed her out of the room but she turned back at the archway exit. "Raven, when things calm down, let's have a girls' night." With a wave, Fallon was gone, bracelets jingling and her skirt floating behind her.

"She's great," Raven said.

Remy chuckled. "She's something, all right. So, how did you sleep?"

As if he didn't know. "Better than I have in years," she admitted. Not wanting to get into how safe she felt with him, she glanced around the kitchen. It didn't look like he'd eaten yet. "Do you have food in the fridge? I'd be happy to make us breakfast."

He raised an eyebrow. "Do you think I'd let you cook?"

His cell rang and he lifted it off the counter. "Just in time." He held up a finger, asking her to wait as he took the call. "Hello?" After listening, he replied. "Send them up, thanks."

"Who's here?" she asked.

He grinned at her, his smile a mix of roguish man and boyish grin. She couldn't resist either.

A few minutes later, they were sitting at the kitchen table, with more choices for breakfast than she'd had in years.

"My God, Remy. What are we going to do with the leftovers?" she asked, as she loaded her plate with scrambled eggs and bacon, one big pancake, and a piece of Belgian waffle.

She picked up the small pitcher holding the syrup. She was mid-pour over the delicious-looking carbs when a realization hit her and she placed the syrup back on the table.

"What's wrong?" Remy asked.

"Why did you order all this food?"

He studied her, eyes crinkled, obviously confused. "Because you had a rough night and I wanted to do something nice for you. What's going through that suspicious mind of yours?" he asked.

She sighed, feeling guilty. "I thought maybe you had news about whether or not Lance had been released early. Not that I have doubts but I thought you were cushioning the blow."

Silence followed her words and she wanted to cringe.

"There's something you need to know about me. If I have something to tell you, I will because I trust you to handle it. *Then* I'll order you pancakes and waffles."

He winked and the knots that had formed in her stomach suddenly eased. His belief in her ability to cope gave her a boost of adrenaline along with the certainty that now was the time to break the news about her weekly plans.

"Remy?" she asked, as she cut up the pancake. "I have plans tonight I can't cancel."

His gaze lifted from his plate and those gorgeous golden eyes met hers. "What plans?"

She swallowed hard. The enjoyment she got from the weekly poetry and short story readings at a nearby coffee shop weren't something she expected him to understand.

"Do you remember when I told you about how I enjoyed Edgar Allan Poe?"

He nodded, the furrow between his brows telling her he had no idea where this explanation was going.

"Well, when I was in college I started writing my own poems and short stories. At first I emulated Poe because my life was so dark at the time. Then, once I moved into my apartment here and things with Lance calmed down, I was able to just write more from the heart. A friend took me with her to a coffee shop that hosted readings every Sunday night and it became a ritual. One I enjoyed."

He'd listened intently, not once interrupting. "So you want to go to a coffee shop tonight?"

She nodded. "It gets crowded but it's important to me."

He lifted a napkin and wiped off his lips. "Raven? Come here."

She rose and walked over to him, shocked when he patted his lap. "Now sit."

More confused than ever, she lowered herself onto his lap. Though she couldn't miss the bulge in his black track pants, she also knew that wasn't why he'd called her over. It was just a side benefit, she mused, and wriggled her ass until his erection nestled between her thighs, leaning her in a more arousing position.

"Behave," he chided. "Now look at me."

She turned her head to face him. Their noses were inches apart and she wanted to taste the maple syrup she smelled on his mouth.

"Why is this the first I'm hearing about this poetry night of yours?"

She blinked. The question might be easy on the surface but the answer forced her to delve deeper. "Because I don't normally share personal things with anyone," she whispered.

He nodded, his lips curving upward in a pleased smiled. "And why are you telling me now?"

She wrinkled her nose, confused. "Because I need you to go with me tonight in case Lance is prowling around." Wasn't that obvious?

"Why else?" he asked, taking her arms and looping them around his neck.

She squirmed at their intimate position which only served to rub his cock against her sex, the wetness between her thighs growing the longer she sat on his lap.

"Raven?" he asked.

"Hmm?" She'd lost all train of thought.

"Why else did you tell me about tonight?"

She stared, lost in the beauty of his handsome features. Could a man be beautiful? She hadn't thought so until she met Remy. "Because I wanted to share a part of my life with you."

The admission shocked her not only because she'd never have told him if he hadn't had her feeling so pliant and safe in his arms. But also because she hadn't realized that truth herself.

"Exactly." That short acknowledgment told her how pleased he was with her answer.

"What are you, like a horse whisperer pulling answers out of me?" she asked.

He shook his head. "I'm a Raven whisperer and I will take you where you want to go tonight as long as you promise me one thing."

"What's that?" she asked, wariness returning.

He ran his knuckles over her cheek. "That you'll stay close to me at all times."

She pursed her lips, knowing he'd find out tonight his request wouldn't be all that easy to do. But since she knew she'd be safe, she was able to make the promise. "I will," she murmured.

Without warning, he shifted her in his lap and suddenly he was standing. She wrapped her legs around his waist, anchoring herself to him. "What are you doing?" she asked.

"We're still friends with benefits, right?"

She nodded, her aching sex keenly aware of which benefit she desired at the moment.

He smiled and pressed a quick kiss to her lips. "Good. Then we're going to exercise some of those benefits. What do you think about spending the day in bed before we have to go out later?"

"Works for me."

A few seconds later, he was tossing her onto the bed and their afternoon began.

Chapter Ten

AGREEING TO TAKE Raven tonight went against Remy's better judgment. But from the second she'd said the weekly event was important to her, he knew he'd give in. Which explained why he was now in a way-too-crowded coffee shop, listening to people read their personal words. Some were poems, others were short stories. Most sounded somewhat autobiographical, even if the meaning was hidden beneath lyrical prose.

Raven had omitted how busy this place would be tonight, no doubt because if she'd told him, he never would have let her come. Keeping her close wasn't easy considering how many people she knew that wanted to corner her and have a word.

For a woman who talked a good game about keeping people at a distance, there was a part of her who liked making friends and discussing things they had in common. When others finished their performance, she clapped and whistled, whether she knew them or not, and made it a point to give them validation during the break.

Despite Remy's unease about her brother stalking

her, he enjoyed watching Raven in her element and wondered if she knew how easily she fit in. How much the individuals in this eclectic group liked her and valued her opinion. Seeing this side of her as opposed to the stiff, keep-to-herself woman at work, was a revelation and showed him who she could be, if only Lance wasn't around to terrorize her.

"Our next presenter is Raven Walsh," Dennis, the manager of the shop, said into the mike.

The Raven who walked up to the makeshift stage wasn't the same woman he employed. At work, she was a no-nonsense bar manager who wore tight jeans and The Back Door T-shirt uniform, hair up in a ponytail. He'd seen her do elegant at Zach and Hadley's wedding. And when she'd dressed tonight, he heard her squeal with excitement from where he was watching television in the den. When he'd popped his head into the bedroom and asked what was up, she'd shooed him away.

A few minutes later, she strode out of the room wearing a peach chiffon skirt that was vintage Fallon, a pair of black leggings beneath it, and matching ballet slippers on her feet. A light gray asymmetric sweater fell off one shoulder and hung long over the skirt. She'd woven a thin, patterned scarf through her hair that she wore loose, and hung down past her shoulders.

Gorgeous and free, that was how he'd describe her.

"When your sister told me about the clothing she'd brought, I was just grateful to have something to wear but she's amazing!" Raven twirled so the skirt floated in the air, then wrapped gently over the leggings.

He chuckled at her enthusiasm but his dick was hard at the thought of lifting that skirt and taking her against the glass window overlooking the city.

He cleared his throat. "I had no idea you shared my sister's taste in clothing."

"I didn't either, but oh my gosh! I'm buying myself fun things first chance I get!" she'd said.

Now they were at the coffee bar, and she stood on the stage, brave, with no uncertainty in sight. This was the woman she'd be once out of Lance's shadow and Remy had every intention of making sure she had that chance.

Even better, the poem she read was about *him*.

Stunned, he listened to poetry he didn't know she could write, more of haiku-type style than anything else. Short bursts of sentences about a man she'd never expected to meet. One out of her league. Out of reach for more reasons than wealth. She spoke about high walls that nobody could breach.

But he wasn't just anyone.

That was when Remy knew. He *was* breaking

through her walls by small degrees and it gave him a spark of hope. True optimism filled him. Then, he leaned back, arms still folded over his chest, and let himself enjoy.

BACK AT REMY'S place, Raven kept busy. She didn't want to allow him time to question her about her poem, not only because her work was deeply personal, but because it had clearly been about him. She hadn't considered the need for him to go with her when she'd written the words.

She'd expected him to question her on the way home but because parking was scarce at the coffee shop, they'd taken an Uber there and then back, and the driver had been chatty.

Once she arrived at Remy's apartment, she went directly to the bathroom and closed the door, washing off her heavier makeup, undressing, and carefully folding the clothing to deal with tomorrow. Fallon's boho style appealed to Raven for the times she wasn't wearing her standard jeans and T-shirt ensemble. Maybe she could ask Remy's sister to go shopping.

Raven pulled on her normal clothing and looked in the mirror, seeing her reflection. Flushed cheeks, bright eyes, and the most surprising part, the excited rush of adrenaline flowing through her. Who was *this* Raven Walsh? And that's when she realized she was changing, trusting Remy, caring for him and his sister, but with Lance out and stalking her, that couldn't happen.

Tears filled her eyes, taking her off guard, but she understood what caused them. This happiness wasn't hers. She couldn't own it because to do so would be to risk the people around her. There would be no shopping with Fallon because… Emily. No way would she allow what had happened to her one-time best friend happen to the bubbly, happy Fallon. Not only would Lance violate her body and hurt her, he'd destroy her spirit.

With the reminder of why Raven couldn't have the life she dreamed of, she sucked in a long breath, pushed all those hopes and dreams down deep, and closed the imaginary box the way she'd learned to compartmentalize.

After she finished in the bathroom, once more dressed in one of Remy's soft T-shirts, she steeled herself and walked into the bedroom.

He'd used the guestroom bathroom and was waiting for her in bed. Raven was prepared for him to want to have sex, especially after that poem in which she bled her feelings all over the coffee shop, and now, she cringed at the memory. All those beautiful feelings? They also had to be stuffed down.

Friends with benefits. Sex. That's all she had to offer and Raven hoped she could manage it without falling harder.

She crawled into the bed and he reached over by his bedside and shut the lamp, plunging them into darkness. His scent enveloped her even before he reached out an arm and pulled her into his embrace. But instead of rolling her over and kissing her as she'd anticipated, he tucked her into him and held her.

"You did wonderful tonight," he said in a gruff voice that awakened all her senses.

"Thank you."

He cleared his throat. "Surprised me, too. I didn't realize you were a poet."

"Mmm. After Lance began terrorizing me in subtle ways, as I grew up, the poems and poets we were learning in school appealed to me. I started to try and emulate them. Hence my love of Poe and others. Soon I had an entire notebook of dark stuff."

A few minutes of quiet followed in which he trailed his rough fingers over her bare arm. She breathed in, closing her eyes and letting his musky scent fill her along with allowing the warmth of his body to coat her in safety.

"Tonight's work wasn't dark," he pointed out.

She stiffened, afraid he'd want to dissect her feelings.

"I liked it," he said, his tone still sexy and rough, but filled with appreciation.

She felt his lips against her hair and then he kissed her neck. Her skin tingled and her sex grew full, her body primed for his. All he had to do was hold her and she became aroused, but right now, her feelings, both physical and emotional, were so much stronger.

Smiling because he couldn't see her expression, she murmured another thank you.

More silence passed and she waited for him to move, act, initiate... something. But he didn't and soon she was groggy and falling into a deep sleep.

He chose that moment to speak again, this time in a whisper. "Thank you for the poem and for trusting me with your feelings. I'll do my best not to abuse the privilege."

The next morning, certain she'd imagined those words, Raven focused on the day ahead. They went into work early so Remy could go over the books and work on some phone calls for his PI job. Raven always had things to keep her busy at the bar.

Stevie arrived shortly after, and they began discussing her friend's nonexistent love life and Stevie bemoaned the lack of good guys out there in the world.

"Ones like your man are certainly few and far between," Stevie said.

Raven shook her head, immediately going into denial mode. "Remy's not my man."

Stevie raised what could only be described as a cynical eyebrow. "I caught you two in a clinch in the hallway on Saturday. Are you really trying to lie to me? I'm hurt, Raven."

Normally, Raven would brush off her friend's words as a joke but the depth of feeling in her tone told Raven that Stevie wasn't kidding.

She turned to face her friend. And that's what Stevie was, Raven realized, despite all attempts to keep her at arm's length. Getting dressed together for Zach and Hadley's wedding, helping one another with their makeup, being there for one another. Wasn't that what girlfriends did?

Raven sighed. "I'm sorry." In need of something to do, she picked up a rag and began to wipe down the bar. "I have reasons for pushing people away. Serious reasons but—" And this next part was hard because Raven wasn't used to letting people in. "I promise to share them with you one day, okay? Just not right now. And not here, while we're at work."

Stevie's pout and hurt expression eased a bit. "We all have our issues but I hope you know you can share yours with me. We're friends."

"I know." Raven forced a smile. "Maybe you can

come by one night and I'll explain." She immediately realized that she was staying with Remy and she'd have to confide in Stevie about that, too. Raven decided she'd cross that bridge when she came to it. Especially since Stevie's eyes had lit up with gratitude and Raven couldn't bring herself to dull it by nixing the idea altogether. Staying and sleeping with the boss. Stevie would just love the information, Raven mused.

"I need to go freshen up. The first customers should be here soon for lunch," Stevie said. When she wasn't serving, she tended bar for extra hours and money.

She strode off and Raven was grateful for the badly needed space. She was even more thankful for managerial busy work as she dove into bookkeeping and forgot about everything else.

After the lunch crowd lessened, Raven sat herself down on a barstool, a large glass of water in front of her. She took a sip and closed her eyes, grabbing a much-needed break.

"Caroline!" A familiar, shrill voice broke into her meditative state.

God, no. Not here. Not now.

She opened her eyes to see her mother standing in front of her, dressed up as if for lunch at The Plaza and not The Back Door bar. Her auburn hair was freshly blow-dried and fluffed, her makeup done to perfection, her lips accentuated with a deep red color, and her Botox prevented her expression from moving.

Rising from her seat, Raven faced her mother. More like the woman who'd raised her. Why give Cassandra a name Raven didn't feel?

"What are you doing here and please don't call me Caroline. You'll confuse people and I've told you I go by my birth name now." Raven would press that issue for as long as it took until she won.

When the Kanes adopted her, Cassandra had changed Raven's name, her first step in molding her into the perfect little girl she'd wanted Raven to be. When Cassandra discovered Raven had a mind of her own and a strong will to be her own person, years later she'd had Cara in order to fulfill the dream. She'd lost on that score too. The only child that was like Cassandra was Lance, something Raven found frightening.

"Are you even listening to me?" Cassandra asked, her voice shrill. "You already *know* why I had to come have a word. Does family mean nothing to you? How could you implicate your brother in a break-in when he's fresh out of prison?" She lowered her voice on the last word as if the fact was too embarrassing to say out loud.

Raven did her best not to roll her eyes. It wasn't like anyone here knew or cared who Cassandra Kane or her precious son Lance were.

"I implicated him because it was obvious who'd broken in." Raven didn't bother to explain how to a woman who wouldn't believe her anyway. "I just told the police what I think is true. It's up to them whether or not they investigate or question him. Besides, if your favorite child is as innocent as you say, they won't bother him again." This time Raven did treat Cassandra to an eye roll.

Undeterred from her rant, Cassandra placed her hands on her hips and went on. "*Caroline*," she emphasized the name. "It's your fault Lance was sent away in the first place. Now you're trying to get him sent to that horrid place again. You've always had an issue with him and for no reason." She shifted her Chanel purse higher on her shoulder.

Raven studied the woman whose house she grew up in, amazed as always that Cassandra truly believed her words.

"I had an issue with Lance because he *terrorized* me. I testified against him because I found him in the middle of assaulting my roommate and about to rape her." Raven's voice rose with every pertinent and awful fact. "And I'd think a woman of your stature and supposed intelligence would know better than to blame the victim, *or* the eyewitness."

"It's your fault!" she said, not for the first time. "We took you in and *you* made Lance crazy, flaunting your body and teasing him, coming into the hallway in a towel, of all things. And you turned Caleb against me. He believes every lie that comes out of your mouth!"

Jesus. The woman was truly insane. And the patrons and employees had stopped what they were doing to watch and listen. Raven was horrified but there was no stopping Cassandra once she got started.

"You have no appreciation, Caroline Kane. I could have left you to rot in foster care but I wanted a little girl and the doctors said I couldn't have children. Then I got *you*. Unruly, disobedient…"

Raven folded her arms across her chest, the only defensive measure she could find. The words were nothing she hadn't heard before and most of it was untrue. She might not have been the daughter Cassandra wanted but she obeyed the rules at home and did what was asked of her. She just hadn't been a frilly, bow-wearing child. Raven normally ignored these tirades but she wasn't alone this time, she was at her place of employment where people knew her. It was embarrassing.

If Cassandra regretted adopting her, Raven felt the same way. She'd have been better off rolling the dice with the foster care system and if her *mother* wasn't so busy going off on Raven and creating a scene, Raven would have told her as much.

But with every jab against her, more people stared, and Raven withdrew further into herself. *This*. This was what had driven her to write down her angry, dark feelings, creating poetry with sad and somber themes. Dark stories… until Remy.

"What the hell is going on?" As if she'd conjured him, Remy joined them, Stevie trailing behind. Raven assumed her friend had let him know what was happening up front.

Cassandra stopped yelling and glanced at Remy. As always, one look at a handsome, younger man, and she morphed into a fake seductress, batting her eyes at him. "I was just giving my daughter a piece of my mind," she said with a sneer on her face.

"I apologize if I made a scene but you see, she's trouble, always has been and—"

"Quiet!" Remy bellowed.

Yep. He raised his normally calm voice and yelled at Cassandra.

Stepping up beside Raven, Remy wrapped an arm around her shoulder and pulled her against him, causing Cassandra's mouth to open in a perfect, shocked O.

"Mrs. Kane, if you don't want me to call the police and have you arrested for creating a disturbance in my place of business, you'll leave. Now."

"But she—"

"Raven did nothing wrong. And if you come near her again, I will personally take her to file a restraining order against you. I have a room full of witnesses, all of whom are her friends and would be only too happy to give a statement."

Cassandra narrowed her gaze. "There is no way you can get a restraining order for a simple disagreement. Besides, I have connections everywhere." She sniffed, raising her nose in the air.

"Try me." Remy's slow smile was scary. "I used to be an NYPD detective and if you think your connections are good, you should see mine. Time to go."

"Mother!" Caleb's voice startled Raven and she stared at her brother in surprise.

"How did you know she was here?" Raven asked.

A grim frown had settled on his lips. "Mother called me to ask if I knew what you'd done to Lance and informed me of her intention to come find you. I got here as fast as I could."

"Caleb, darling, I know you have a relationship with Caroline, so could you *please* try and talk sense into her?" she begged, once again turning on her fake charm.

"Her name is Raven." Caleb winked at Raven, his expression reassuring. "Don't worry. I'll get her out of here."

He grasped his mother's elbow and led her out of

the restaurant, Cassandra complaining the entire way. But her absence didn't make her embarrassment disappear. Although Raven did her best to ignore what others said, thought, or did, Cassandra's tantrum in front of her colleagues had been appalling.

"Come on." Remy's voice caused her tension to ease.

She'd forgotten he had an arm around her, one he now used to guide her back toward his office.

Once they were inside, Remy shut the door and Raven sat down on the seat across from his desk.

He lowered himself into the chair beside her and took her hand. "You okay?" Frown lines had settled in the creases of his eyes and she hated how worried he was for her.

She blew out a deep breath. "A little shaken, to be honest. She took me off guard by coming here and those verbal blows hit me where it hurt."

"I didn't catch anything but those last awful comments," he said, rubbing his thumb back and forth over the top of her hand.

"But I know without hearing it all, she was out of line."

"Except nobody listening would know that. I'm the manager here. These people are supposed to respect me and do as I say. Meanwhile…"

"No." His voice was curt and to the point. "Not

only are these people, you mentioned, employees, we're all tight. Like a family. Trust me, they will automatically be concerned about you and think Cassandra was an arrogant, snooty—"

A knock interrupted his list of impolite words to describe Cassandra Kane, and Raven was smiling when Remy called out, "Come in!"

The door opened and Caleb stood in the doorway. "Am I interrupting?"

She shook her head. "Not at all. Come in. I assumed you'd be taking Cassandra home."

Caleb shook his head. "No need. She took a driver. She was still complaining when I made sure she sat down in the back of the vehicle and closed her in. I made certain to watch the car drive off." He closed the door behind him and walked over to the desk, leaning against the metal frame, facing Raven and Remy. "I'm sorry."

"Don't you dare," she warned her brother. "Her behavior is not on you."

He nodded. "How are *you*?"

Now that she'd had time to calm down and get over the shock of Cassandra's visit, Raven realized Remy had a point. As much as his mother's behavior wasn't Caleb's fault, Raven's friends would take what had happened in stride… though she knew they'd be curious.

"I'm better, thanks. I shouldn't have let her get to me." There was no point in elaborating again on why she had.

Caleb smiled but it didn't reach his eyes. "Yeah, but that's not easy. Mother knows where to aim her arrows. Now, on to more important things. Are we still on for dinner? Your nephew was asking me all morning if we were seeing Aunt Raven tonight."

"I wouldn't miss a date with my little man." Raven was excited about the evening ahead. "Do you mind if I bring a guest?" More like a bodyguard, but she wouldn't insult Remy by calling him that, and her gaze slid to his to find his warm stare watching her.

"Of course not. But I need to get going. I'll see you at our usual spot?"

"Yes." She pushed herself up from the chair, dislodging Remy's hand, and she immediately felt the loss. It wasn't sexual either, it was the certainty that this man could protect her. That he wanted to.

And she didn't quite know what to do with that.

Remy stood as well and said goodbye to Caleb.

Once her brother had left, Remy turned to face her. "Dinner with your nephew, huh?"

"Think you can handle it?" she teased, feeling lighter than she had since Cassandra had shown up.

"If you're going to be there, I know I can."

Chapter Eleven

REMY AND RAVEN went straight from work to the restaurant in Brooklyn because Owen ate dinner early. It wasn't a long trip and Remy drove them in his car.

He'd never been to the Harlem Shake restaurant before but he discovered they had another establishment at 124th Street in Harlem, uptown. And after eating there, he understood the appeal for kids. The décor was 1950s diner chic, with a lot of chrome and swirling stools that Owen had a blast using.

Letting him order a root beer float kept him busy slurping and playing with the straw while the grownups talked. Early in the meal, Raven seemed uneasy, glancing around and looking over her shoulder. Remy already had an eye out for anyone or anything unusual, but his instincts hadn't buzzed with awareness. Still, he could sense her discomfort.

Caleb was smart and steered the conversation away from his mother and brother and onto other things, and soon Raven had settled down and was focused on her nephew.

"Hey, buddy. Can I have a sip of your float?"

Owen's lips turned down in a pout. "But I only have a drop left. See?" He pointed to the tall glass which was still half full.

Matching his pout by pursing her lips, Raven folded her arms across her chest. "But I don't have any more water and I'm thirsty." She met the little boy's gaze in a staring contest Remy had no doubt she'd win.

"Owen, what did I say about sharing?" Caleb asked in a calm, easy dad-like voice. It reminded Remy of his father's way of admonishing his kids without yelling.

"Fine." Owen's bottom lip pushed out even farther.

Grinning, Raven took her own straw and stuck it into the drink and took a long sip. The straw was clear and it was obvious to the grown-ups, at least, she hadn't pulled up any liquid, saving it all for her nephew.

"Yum!" she said, as she lifted her head. "Best root beer float ever. Thank you so much for sharing. You're the man!" She held up her hand for a high five, which Owen gladly gave, smacking her hand with his, grinning the entire time, his upset already forgotten.

"Want to share my fries?" She pushed her plate full of French fries loaded with cheese toward him.

The kid had been eyeing them since they'd been delivered to the table. "Yes! I forgot to ask Dad if I could have them with my burger. You're the best, Aunt Raven!"

He went to town on the fries, leaving the adults grinning at one another and Remy amazed at her way with children.

On the drive home, he said as much.

She shrugged. "Owen makes it easy. He's a really good kid."

He glanced at her profile. God, she was beautiful, with her delicate profile, porcelain skin, and plush lips. "Do you ever think about having children of your own?" he asked, keeping conversation light.

She spun to face him. "And how would that work?" she asked in a bitter tone. "I'd be giving Lance another target, for one thing. And what if he tried something and I had to pick up and leave town? How easy would that be with a kid?" She pulled in a shaky breath. "No, Remy, I've never thought about having kids of my own," she said as she did a full-body turn and stared out the passenger-side window.

Fuck. So much for light conversation, he thought, his stomach cramping at his carelessly asked question and her pain-filled words.

"I wasn't thinking. I'm sorry."

She sighed and turned back toward him. "It's fine. I just… yeah, I'd like kids. I just don't see it in the cards for me," she said, and was silent for the rest of the trip.

The quiet that followed gave him time to think about their evening. Raven had a good time with her brother but until she'd focused on Owen, she'd been nervous and jittery.

"Was something wrong earlier?" he asked, breaking the stillness and silence.

"What do you mean?" she asked.

He thought back to the crowded restaurant and the way she'd been craning her neck and looking around. He hadn't said anything at the time because any question would lead to a discussion of Lance and Remy hadn't wanted to upset Caleb's son.

"When we first arrived at the restaurant you kept looking around. I had my eye on things, but I didn't notice anything wrong." He paused, then asked, "Did you?"

She rubbed her hands on her black jeans. "Well, to be honest, I felt like someone was watching me but…" She shook her head. "I discounted the possibility because we were in Brooklyn, not the city close to where I live, and everyone else seemed calm. Especially you, so I chalked it up to my imagination."

Remy had just pulled into the underground parking garage where he lived, turned into his designated spot, and cut the engine.

"Besides," she continued. "Caleb always says

Lance wouldn't do anything with Owen around but…
I'm not so sure. I've warned him about trusting that
twin bond, and I've been adamant that I don't think
Lance is capable of feeling what Caleb does. That's
why I never agreed to live with them. I wouldn't ever
put that sweet boy in harm's way."

"I agree with you."

"You do?" She sounded relieved.

He nodded. "And just because I didn't notice anyone doesn't mean I'd discount your intuition. Always
trust your instincts," he told her, vowing silently to up
his game. Watch more closely.

She let out a long, pained sigh. "I don't think I
should see Caleb and Owen for a while." Disappoint-
ment and hurt filled her voice. "God, I hate that Lance
is in control of my life." She fumbled for the door
handle, clearly eager to escape the confines of the
vehicle.

"Raven, wait."

She turned and the agony in her contorted expression gutted him.

Reaching out, he stroked her cheek. "We'll figure
something out, okay?"

She nodded and he only hoped he could live up to
the trust in her eyes.

Chapter Twelve

THE NEXT POETRY slam occurred a week later and despite Raven's nerves about attending with a packed store full of people, she wanted to go. Although she didn't have anything of her own to read, she wanted to go support a friend. She'd already called Caleb and canceled her weekly dinners with him and Owen, and she'd made him promise to tell her nephew she'd make it up to him. She only wished she knew when that would be possible.

Her next call had been to her sister, letting Cara know about their mother's visit and making her aware that Lance was stalking Raven. Though Remy hadn't noticed him, Raven was certain he was around. Somewhere. The only reason she would even consider going tonight was because she'd have Remy by her side. She doubted he'd be understanding and had stalled bringing it up with him.

But now, as she woke up naked in his arms, she realized the day had arrived and she had no choice. She was curled around him, her cheek on his shoulder, facing him, her knee lifted and resting over his warm body.

Knowing what she needed to ask, she wasn't above playing dirty. Besides, she thought, as she shifted her hips, moaning softly as her sex rubbed against his hard thigh, they'd both enjoy her seduction. She lowered her leg so she stretched beside him and slid a hand over his hips, grasping his cock in her hand.

Since she'd been staying there, they'd developed a healthy sex life. One she still insisted was a friends-with-benefits arrangement. It was the only way she could justify getting closer to him—because he was helping her with the Lance situation.

Her brother wasn't something she wanted to think about while she was rubbing herself against Remy, all the while pumping her hand up and down his shaft and feeling his erection grow thicker in her hand.

"Raven," he said in that rough morning voice she loved. "Is my girl horny?"

My girl. All her lady bits tingled at his use of that expression. One she wished could be true. But she didn't see Lance going anywhere anytime soon. Not if Cassandra had her say. She'd do anything to keep her baby boy, as she thought of him, protected and out of prison. *Stop!* she internally screamed at herself.

Drawing a breath, she refocused on the more enjoyable man before her. "Yes, Remy, I'm horny," she admitted.

With a low chuckle, he lifted his body and in seconds, had her pinned beneath him, his cock nestled exactly where she wanted it. Her sex grew heavy and wet, desire filling her and pushing all other thoughts aside. Except the awareness that yes, she needed something from him he wouldn't like.

His lips came down hard on hers and she moaned into his mouth. Arching her lower body, she raised her hips and wrapped her legs around his, anchoring herself to him. The kiss went on for a while, his teeth pulling at her lower lip, tongue soothing the ache he created, and his hands roaming over her skin. And that thick cock rubbing against her pussy.

Before she could think of what she wanted to do or say next, he'd managed to free himself from her grasp, positioned himself at her entrance, and slid home. He filled her, not with a hard, fast thrust but a slow, easy glide that said more than she was ready to accept. He rocked his hips, their bodies gliding against each other's, the friction delicious, and his long cock managing to rub over just the right spot.

"Remy," she moaned, unable to hold back. "More."

"Anything you want, baby."

She knew this was the moment she should stop him, turn this situation into a teasing one that let her ask for something in return for letting him continue. He'd be annoyed. She'd coax and cajole him into saying yes to taking her tonight and they'd both finish with explosive orgasms. A win-win.

Except what he was doing to her body included her emotions and she closed her eyes, lost as he continued to undulate his hips and make love to her until she was soaring in the clouds and screaming his name.

He hadn't come yet and he picked up his pace. "Look at me, beautiful."

Raven forced her heavy-lidded gaze open and stared into those golden-brown orbs. Only then did he begin to fuck her, slamming into her over and over again. He was a master at finding her G-spot and when he shifted position, she began to rise again, pleasure and waves of need pouring through her until finally he gave one last thrust. He hit the perfect point again and as she came, so did he with a growl of satisfaction, hips sliding in and out until he finally settled inside her and collapsed, his breath warm on her neck.

A few minutes later, they were sweaty and damp as he held her tight. "I could wake up like this every morning," he said, satisfaction filling his tone.

"Mmm." So could she but she held back the admission. Anything that indicated long term was impossible and hurt too much to think about.

"Raven?"

Something worrisome in his tone had her stiffening and paying attention. "What is it?" she asked.

"We didn't use a condom."

She blinked in surprise. She'd been diligent in including that added layer of protection with him. "I—"

"It's okay," he said, stroking her hair. "I'm certain I'm clean. Recent checkup and blood work," he told her.

She relaxed against him. "Good. Me too, and I'm on the pill."

So the chances of anything going wrong were a narrow one percent. She remembered asking the doctor about the best method of birth control when she became sexually active and that slim number had stuck with her.

With that out of the way, she closed her eyes and thought about the feel of him bare inside her and smiled.

"You look satisfied," he said.

She opened her eyes to find him staring at her, a self-satisfied grin on his face. "That's because I am. But don't let it go to your head, you arrogant man."

She waited through his low laugh before speaking again. "Remy, I need to ask you something."

"What is it?" His fingers were tangling in her hair and she enjoyed the slight pull at her scalp, finding it arousing.

But they were not going for round two. Not until

she'd settled her evening plans.

"Tonight is another poetry night at the coffee house."

He stiffened beside her. "No."

"But—"

"Every time you go anywhere but the bar or this apartment, you feel like someone's watching you. There's no reason to put you in jeopardy."

She sighed and having expected the argument, was ready with one of her own. "Do you remember Angelica? Angel? The girl I introduced you to at the last event?"

"Yeah."

She pushed off him and sat up, curling her legs beneath her, unconcerned she was naked. His gaze, on the other hand, settled on her breasts and she didn't bother covering them.

"Well, she's young and tonight is the first time she's going to get up onstage. She needs me there for moral support and I promised I wouldn't let her down."

A displeased sound rumbled in Remy's chest. "Lance doesn't care that you have a soft, giving heart. If he wants to rattle you, he will do his damnedest to frighten you. Worst case, he gets his hands on you. So no." He pushed himself up against the pillows and headboard, arms folded across his broad chest.

"Are you doubting your ability to protect me? Because if so, maybe it's time to call in the bodyguards you mentioned you hired for Emily."

Soon after her apartment window had been broken, Remy had sat Raven down and told her Garrett checked on Emily. She was aware of Lance's release and was taking precautions. Knowing that wouldn't be enough for Raven, Remy had hired Alpha Security to keep an eye on the woman from afar. She'd had been so grateful, she'd broken down and cried.

Remy narrowed his gaze. "Don't try and manipulate me," he muttered. "Especially not when it comes to your safety."

She let out a sigh. "I'm sorry. It's just that Angel is only seventeen and she's about to age out of foster care. These nights mean so much to her and she finally worked up the courage to participate."

"Raven," he said in a warning tone.

She clasped her hands in front of her in a praying gesture. "Please? We'll go, see Angel, I'll let her know how well she did, and then we can leave. I'm sorry for what I said. I trust you to protect me," she added. And she did or she wouldn't think of attending.

"You're killing me." He shook his head and closed his eyes. "Tell me one thing."

She nodded, eager to answer him because she sensed he was weakening. "Sure."

"Did you wake me up and seduce me in order to get your way when my defenses were down?" His knowing gaze bore into hers.

Shoulders drooping, she nodded. "It started out that way but the second I touched you, I forgot all about having an agenda. I wanted you," she said in a husky voice.

"Dammit, Raven." He met her gaze and she hoped it was resignation she saw in his eyes and tight expression.

"So… you'll take me?"

"You don't go anywhere where I can't see you. If you need the ladies' room, I'm standing outside. I mean it."

She exhaled long and hard. "Okay. I promise." Relieved and happy, she dove over him, assuming what she'd begun to think of as her spider monkey position, hugging him as she wrapped herself around him.

"What am I going to do with you?" he muttered into her hair.

She couldn't hold back her smile. "I can think of a few things."

Next thing she knew, he was inside her again and nothing around her existed or mattered but Remy.

THAT NIGHT, REMY was on high alert at the coffee shop. He still couldn't believe how the little minx had gone about convincing him to take her.

His gaze darted from the entrance around to every corner of the room. No Lance.

Though she'd come to his apartment with the clothes on her back, Remy had gone upstairs to her place one night while she was busy at the bar, and packed up clothing and personal items to bring home. He thought surrounding her with her own things would help ease her anxiety. Raven was grateful but to his surprise, she'd also ordered items online that were more like his sister's taste and tonight's outfit was a new version of Fallon's boho look.

Raven dressed in a new flowy skirt, this one a bright orange, leggings to keep her skin warm underneath, a navy sweater with open shoulders and a pair of white Chucks.

He had the sense she was coming into her own without realizing it and her need to be there for the young girl she'd mentioned was the deciding factor for Remy in agreeing to come tonight. He couldn't be the reason she let the girl down.

He leaned against a wall at the coffee shop, drink in one hand. He'd chosen a spot with a good vantage point to look around and one with a direct view of the entrance. Raven had promised to stick close and let the people she knew drift toward her to say hello instead of him having to scope her out as she moved around the crowded room.

Since this wasn't his first time there, familiar faces said hi to him and he nodded or smiled back. Remy wasn't an antisocial guy but he had an important focus tonight and he didn't want to be distracted because he was deep in conversation.

Raven was more jittery this evening than last Sunday, which surprised him since she wasn't going onstage. She bounced lightly on her Chucks, looking around.

"If you see him, all you need to do is tell me. He won't get near you. Not with me around," he assured her.

She tilted her head up to meet his gaze. "I'm not worried about Lance. Angel isn't here and I hope she didn't decide to blow the night off."

He couldn't control the warmth filling his chest at her response, nor did he want to. She was everything warm and giving and the deeper she let him in, the more he liked what he saw.

"I'm sure Angel will show up." He hoped he was right because he had a feeling Raven would be devastated if she didn't. "Do you have any way to reach her?" he asked.

Raven shook her head. "She never gave me her

number."

"Raven." A young guy wearing a beanie with long hair walked up to her and engaged her in conversation, which gave Remy a chance to look around. To see if there was any sign of Lance.

The early, mingling part of the evening continued in the same way, with Raven worrying about her friend and Remy's concern more focused on her brother. And he wasn't talking about Caleb.

"She's here!" Raven exclaimed in an excited voice. She took two steps away from him and he grasped her elbow, preventing her from leaving.

"Let her come to you, remember?"

His gut told him it was time for Lance to make a move. The bastard had broken in through her bedroom window, and had obviously been tailing her as she went to dinner with Caleb, and then at the last poetry slam. Lance would be dying to step things up again, scare her and receive an adrenaline rush-filled jolt of satisfaction, knowing he'd gotten to her.

"You made it!" Raven exclaimed, relief filling her eyes.

"I'm so sorry I'm late," a young girl with long blonde hair said as she rushed over. She pulled a hat off her head and tucked it into a worn tote bag. "My train stopped and I had to wait until it got moving again." She panted, out of breath.

"Relax," Raven said, touching Angel's shoulder. "It hasn't even started yet."

Nodding, she rubbed her obviously cold hands together. After a few minutes, she removed her jacket and placed it on a chair near where Raven and Remy had put theirs.

The owner, who Remy recognized, stepped up to the mike and the night began. He listened to the poems with half an ear and kept an eye on the door at the same time.

"I'm ready. I can do this," Angel said to Raven, who still stood beside her.

Raven smiled wide. "You can. Now go knock 'em dead."

"Come with me!" The young girl grabbed her hand and pulled.

Raven's gaze shot from Angel to Remy. "Please? I'll just be near the stage and you can watch me the entire time."

He groaned. The fact was, he had a view of the entrance and the stage was nearby. "Fine, but do not go out of my sight. No bathroom, nothing."

"Yes, sir." With a cheeky grin, she saluted him.

He leaned forward and whispered in her ear, "Do that again and I'll be more than happy to kiss that smile off your face."

Cheeks pink, she turned and followed Angel.

The young girl's turn came soon and she clomped onstage in her heavy boots. Angel's words came from both the heart and experience about her time on the street, her feelings of solitude, and was filled with enough emotion to give Remy a lump in his throat. She ended to a standing ovation and ran off the stage, giving Raven a hug.

Afterward, Raven started to walk back toward him. Without warning, her expression morphed into one of horror and fear. Her eyes grew wide, mouth parted in shock. She glanced from him to the side door and pointed, gesturing wildly.

Remy turned his head but all he saw was an entrance to the hallway leading to the bathrooms. And the fire exit.

"Why didn't you go after him?" she asked, slamming into Remy and wrapping herself around him. He loved when she did it with exuberance. Not so much now when she was afraid.

"I didn't see him," he said, anger at himself for somehow missing the bastard settling like lead in Remy's stomach.

"I saw Lance. I swear!"

He moved her away from him, keeping his hands on her shoulders. "Shh. I believe you."

But Lance was smart. He was following her, and even Remy, for all his experience, hadn't seen a tail.

Lance had picked a hidden exit that Remy scoped out last time but the door had been permanently locked, according to the manager. Remy had asked.

No doubt Lance had gotten in by charming a female employee. It didn't matter enough for Remy to bother asking around. Raven wouldn't be coming back here.

"Let's go home." He grasped her hand, intending to keep her tight against him until they were in an Uber.

"What if he's outside when we leave?"

Remy groaned. "He won't be. He accomplished his main goal tonight. He rattled you. Now you'll be looking over your shoulder everywhere you go."

"How can you be so sure you're right?"

"Experience," he said grimly. His time as a detective and later, looking for missing women, had taught him more than he wanted to know about the mind of a sociopath. "As for Lance, knowing you're wound up tight and thinking about him will keep him satisfied until... I mean, for a while."

Thankfully she didn't ask *until what*. And Remy didn't let himself think about the answer. Because, he thought, as he pulled out his cell to arrange for a ride, they wouldn't be in the city when Lance was ready to make his move.

Chapter Thirteen

NOW THAT RAVEN was safe in Remy's apartment, she'd calmed down, certain she'd overreacted to seeing Lance at the coffee shop. After all, she'd been safe, surrounded by people, and he couldn't have hurt her even if he'd wanted to. But the moment she'd seen him for the first time, her gaze meeting eyes that were so similar to Caleb's but lacked the warmth and humanity of the brother she loved, she'd panicked. As Remy said, she'd fed his need to scare her. But she was safe. At least for a while.

"Raven, I need you to pack your things." Remy entered the room, a large suitcase in hand. "We're leaving town."

She blinked, stunned. "What? No. I have work. *You* have work."

"I've got that covered. I put Stevie in charge of the bar and we have Pamela for the restaurant," he said of the sub-manager under Raven.

She blew out a breath and did her best not to engage Remy in an argument when he obviously had a plan she wasn't aware of. So she'd talk rationally, then she'd engage. Hadn't she said she didn't want to run but live her life? But she couldn't deny she was scared of Lance, worried he was escalating or planned to. Remy might be a detective but she'd watched enough television shows and real true crime documentaries to know Remy was right.

"Where are we going?" she asked, as he lifted the empty but large piece of luggage, placing it on the bed.

"My family has a compound on Cape Cod."

"Of course they do," she muttered. The Kanes had money and were wealthy in their world but the Sterling financial situation was beyond her wildest imaginings. Maybe when she'd lived in Cassandra and her father's home in Chappaqua she might have felt a little more comfortable at the idea of going to a *compound* but now? She'd been supporting herself on her salary and pinching pennies like the average New Yorker for so long, Remy's type of money intimidated her.

Still... "I really want to argue with you. A part of me says I should stay and make a stand but the part of me that panicked when I saw Lance tells me to pack up and go. No more questions asked."

He strode over and cupped her cheek in his hand. "I couldn't handle it if anything happened to you. So if you're waffling on your decision, can you do this for me?"

She swallowed hard. Put that way, how could she resist? She'd never had anyone worry or care about her the way Remy did except Caleb and Cara. But Caleb was her brother with a child to be concerned about, and Cara was still, for most purposes, a teenager who focused only on herself.

Except, her sister had called this morning because she'd heard about their mother's visit and public spectacle. She was worried and wanted her to know she was Team Raven. Raven smiled at the thought of her caring sibling. They were the two reasons being adopted by the Kanes had been a good thing. Three when she counted her little nephew. They'd want her to go with Remy and keep herself safe.

"Raven? Where did you go?" Remy asked, his deep voice bringing her back to the here and now.

"Just thinking," she murmured. "Okay, we'll leave town."

His eyes lit up and that sexy mouth lifted in a grin. "You'll love the Cape."

"Even in the winter?" she asked.

"Especially in the winter. Now pack."

WHILE RAVEN PACKED, she called her sister and Caleb to let them know she was leaving town. Both agreed it was a good idea and appreciated that she had Remy to look out for her. As an independent woman, normally Raven would argue that she could take care of herself. Just not when it came to Lance.

A little while later, they were on their way in Remy's large SUV. He was alert and diligent, often looking in the rearview mirror, and yes, even taking a circuitous route around the city before leaving town. No doubt to lose any potential tail.

The adrenaline rush of seeing Lance in person had worn off and exhaustion claimed her. Raven dozed as they drove in the dark of night to Cape Cod. She woke up to the feel of the truck coming to a stop, and Remy opening his window to press a series of numbers into a keypad to open the gate.

Despite the outdoor light fixtures lining the driveway, it was difficult to see her surroundings and she had a feeling she'd be blown away in the morning.

A Porsche SUV was parked in the driveway.

"Shit," Remy muttered.

She glanced at his profile. "What's wrong?"

He cut the engine. "Looks like we have company. That's Dex's car."

Despite having been around the Sterling family the times they came to the bar, Raven didn't know any of them well. Dex, the ex-pro-football player, always seemed like a fun guy. Always upbeat and friendly.

"Well, I look forward to getting to know him a little." She opened her car door and slid out, meeting

Remy around the back. Out of nowhere, a large black dog came bounding toward them, the exuberance in the animal easy to see.

"Pogo!" Remy said in a deep voice, and the dog came to a skidding stop in front of them, tongue lolling out of his mouth, and snow on his nose.

"Pogo?" Laughing, she pet his head.

"He belongs to the groundskeeper who lives in a house on the property. To hear him tell it, this guy loved to hop when he was a puppy."

"Like a pogo stick," she said, understanding.

"You're not afraid of him," an unfamiliar voice said.

She turned to see Dex had walked out of the house, joining them. Raven preferred Remy's looks but Dex was a handsome man. From what the press said, women loved him and being a playboy jock, Dex loved them right back.

"Raven, right?"

She nodded. "Hi, Dex."

"What are you doing here?" Remy asked, pulling a suitcase out of the truck.

"Nice way to greet me, asshole. Good to see you too," Dex said with a grin on his face.

Remy rolled his eyes.

"I have big meetings next week and I decided to take a couple of days to unwind." Dex unconsciously put a hand on the dog's big head as he spoke.

Remy took another, smaller suitcase out of the SUV, hit a button and the back door lowered and latched. "Do you think you'll take the job?" He turned to Raven. "Dex has been offered a major network broadcasting gig for Sunday Night Football."

"That's amazing."

Dex merely shrugged, humble. "I need to decide how I feel about the travel before I accept or not."

"That makes sense," she murmured.

"Find an apartment?" Remy asked.

He laughed. "I need to decide where I want to live. Uptown, downtown, midtown."

"Jesus. I don't get why you let your place in the city go. At least you'd have had a home base."

"I have Dad's house and he's happy to let me live there. Besides, this way if I hook up with someone, it has to be at their place. It's easier for me to get out the next morning instead of having to make them leave. It's not always easy to be me."

Raven grinned.

"This guy," Remy said with a shake of his head. "Now, can we go inside? It's freezing."

They trudged up to the house, the dog following close behind.

Dex stopped. "Go home," he said to the big, black dog.

After giving him a soulful look, the dog bounded off, for home, she assumed. "He's well trained."

"Brian takes in dogs and trains them, too. The grounds are big enough. Let's get going. Remy's got thin blood," Dex said.

Remy smacked him lightly on the head and they all headed inside.

Raven glanced around, taking in the rustic feel of the cabin-like house that featured modern accessories and amenities. Despite the huge property and the idea of so many surrounding homes, Raven felt at home here.

She pulled off her jacket and laid it over the tallest piece of luggage. The guys did the same, stripping off their jackets. Remy wore a sweatshirt and a pair of faded jeans that she'd already noticed clung lovingly to his ass. An ass she liked to squeeze when he was on top of her and thrusting deep.

She cleared her throat. "Is it okay if I wander and check out the house?" she asked, eager to get away.

"Make yourself at home," the man who starred in her dirty dreams said. "I'll hang out with Dex for a while."

Relieved Remy hadn't noticed the heavy flush on her cheeks, she nodded and took off to check out the massive house, leaving the men alone.

★　★　★

REMY AND DEX ended up in the family room. The house had a slight chill and Remy immediately decided he'd be making a fire so he could sit in here and have Raven snuggled close.

"I said I'd wait and decide if you need a lecture. You do. So… another damsel in distress?" Dex asked.

Remy stiffened. There was no equating Raven with any woman in his past. "It's not like that."

Dex raised an eyebrow. "Then what is it like because as I recall, every woman you've been with since Mom died was someone who needed you in some way. You need to save them."

Frowning, Remy glared at his brother. "I don't have a savior complex and Raven is different."

"Oh, so she's not here because you're protecting her from her psychotic brother?"

Without answering, Remy walked over to the French doors and looked out onto the rolling lawn behind, covered in light snow. Knowing Dex would give him this time to think, he took advantage.

As much as Remy resented his brother's words, he knew Dex meant well. The truth was, their mother's death had been the catalyst for Remy going into police work and joining up with Zach when that job became stale. True, he'd met his ex-wife when she'd been the victim of a mugging and stabbing. She'd needed him and he liked being needed. Liked knowing he could help her where he couldn't with his mother. They were married after six months.

What could Remy say? He'd been young, out of the academy only three years, and eager to settle down. He'd come home one night after being grazed by a bullet and bandaged at the hospital. The sight had awakened Sadie from her fog, as he now saw it. She'd left him a short time afterward, unable to handle the danger inherent in his job. Why she couldn't have realized that *before* they got married was beyond him, but all victims handled the aftermath differently.

Remy thought about the women he dated afterward and turned to meet his patient brother's gaze. "Fine. So maybe I do have a complex," he muttered. "And you and Fallon talk too much," he said, knowing his siblings had likely discussed the situation since they were the only two people in the family who knew about Raven's stalker issue.

"Fallon loves you and is worried about you. And frankly, so am I. When you told me you were into Raven…" He tilted his head toward the main part of the house where Raven was wandering. "I figured it'd be short term and fizzle out. But you brought her to the family compound?"

"Because I need to keep her safe and with me. And

before you give me that look, the situation is different from Sadie or anyone else. *Raven* is different." He'd known it from the moment they met. Maybe she needed his help now but that hadn't been the reason he'd fallen for her.

"So she's not just another one of your mysteries you like to solve?"

Remy shook his head. "Dammit, Dex. Stop trying to psychoanalyze me."

His brother merely grinned.

"Fine. Raven was a mystery, too." But not any longer. He was drawn to everything about her.

Her beauty was one thing and wasn't just surface deep. The more he got to know her, the more he liked what was inside. Her bond with the family she loved, Cara, Caleb, and Owen, resembled Remy's relationship with his family. She liked to help people like Angel; they had that in common.

"Dex, if you can't trust me when I say Raven is unlike any other woman I've met or been with, then I'm done talking."

"Relax," Dex said. "I was just making sure you were in deep for the right reasons. From the little I've seen, I like her for you."

Remy's shoulders lowered, his guard coming down. He hadn't realized how angry Dex's questions had made him but he realized now why his brother had pushed so hard. "I get it. When you fall, I'll be right there making sure she's the right woman for you, too."

Dex's eyes opened comically wide. "That won't be happening. I'm happy with my life the way it is."

Remy let out a loud laugh. "If you say so." Dex had a traumatic past. Between losing his parents and later his second mother, it had caused him to keep women at arm's length. But Remy had no doubt the right female would knock the playboy right out of him and make Dex Sterling a one-woman man.

"I need to bring the suitcases upstairs," Remy said.

"And I need to get going. It's late. Say goodbye to Raven for me," Dex said.

"I will… but why don't you wait until morning to make the long trip? It's dark and the roads are empty," Remy asked.

"Aww, are you worried about me?" Dex strode over and pulled Remy into a brotherly hug.

"I'm always worried about you, asshole."

Stepping back, Dex yawned, mouth wide open. "That actually sounds like a good idea. But I'll probably be gone by the time you and your *guest* make it out of bed in the morning." His words, like his wagging eyebrows, were deliberately suggestive.

"Go away."

Then, laughing, Dex did just that.

Chapter Fourteen

AFTER DEX HAD gone to his room, Remy remained in the family room, thinking more about what Dex had said, about Remy and his past, the women he'd dated, and especially the one he'd married. Had he been drawn to Sadie's vulnerability? Yes. He liked women with a soft inside but he'd quickly realized he preferred them with a hard-core outside, too. And Raven? She was as strong as they came or else she'd have picked up and run far from Lance as she could.

Though Dex's words and concern came from a good place, Remy was certain. His feelings for Raven were deeper and more meaningful than for anyone in his past. And she was not just his usual, damsel-in-distress M.O.

As he came to that conclusion, she joined him, walking into the large den. It had to be massive to accommodate his big family.

"Hey, did you like the house?" he asked.

She nodded, eyes glittering. "It's incredible. Did your parents own it when you were a kid?"

"Sure did. This is the best place for four rambunctious boys and their sister to play."

Her smile seemed wistful and he decided to break whatever thoughts had her frowning. Probably ones about her childhood that centered on her asshole brother.

"So, Dex went to bed. He plans to be out of here early tomorrow morning. But he said to say goodbye."

"That's nice." She glanced away, then raised her arms over her head and stretched, the hem of her shirt lifting up and revealing an enticing strip of bare skin. "Despite sleeping most of the ride here, I'm tired."

Walking over to her, he tugged on the bottom of her shirt. "Let's go upstairs. You can take a warm bath and relax, then get some sleep."

And while she was doing that, maybe he'd take care of his dick, which was hard from watching her stretch and push her breasts against the long-sleeve T-shirt. With all that was going on in her life, he didn't want to push for sex and his cock wasn't happy with him.

"That sounds perfect," she said.

They walked out to the foyer. Remy grabbed the larger suitcase and let her take the smaller carry-on. She followed him up the stairs and to the bedroom that had always been his. When they were kids, he and Dex had twin beds on opposite sides of the room. As they grew into adults, Dex took his own room and their father, with Lizzie's help, redid Remy's with a king-size bed.

"You can unpack now or later," he said to Raven after putting the larger suitcase on the mattress.

"Will we be here long enough to bother?" she asked, walking around the bedroom, taking in the light wood furniture, modern abstract photograph on the wall, and yes, the large bed.

"I wish I knew." Up until now, he hadn't been informing her of his daily calls to Garrett, preferring to let her live in peace. Or as much peace as she could find with Lance out of prison.

He sighed. "I've been speaking to Garrett. My last call to him was while you were packing up your toiletries."

She paused in the midst of unzipping the luggage. "What did he say? Is he going to question Lance again?" Her voice lifted with hope.

"No," he said, hating to disappoint her. "He got nowhere regarding him breaking your window. There were no prints. Lance denied being anywhere near the apartment and as you know, your mother provided an alibi." As a result, the case had been labeled an ordinary break-in, one foiled by the alarm system scaring off the would-be intruder.

Raven lowered herself onto the light gray comforter. "What about Lance showing up tonight where I just happened to be?"

"Unfortunately, he's done nothing illegal. Not unless you have a restraining order and without solid proof of harassment, no judge will sign off on one."

She clenched her hands in frustration, her knuckles turning white. "It's so unfair."

He stepped closer and put his hands on her shoulders. "Lance will slip up. Even the smartest criminal always does." What neither of them asked was just how long it might take. Remy knew they couldn't hide out here forever.

Their trip here was supposed to give her some time to relax and breathe. "Why don't you go take a nice, luxurious bath? There are soaps and other... girly things in Fallon's room. I'll go grab some."

His words broke the tension and Raven smiled. "Girly things?"

He lifted his shoulder. "I don't know. I think they're called, what? Bath bombs?"

"Oooh, I love those but I haven't indulged in a while."

He stepped back, giving her breathing room. "Then go ahead and do it now. I can unpack for us if you don't mind me going through your things."

She let out a light, tinkling laugh. "Suit yourself. It's not like you're going to find sexy, frilly underwear or teddies." She pushed to her feet and he left the room, walking to his sister's bedroom and returning with a handful of girly things and placing them on the bed.

Raven was digging through the suitcase and as he walked in, she pulled out a pair of plain, white silk panties and one of his T-shirts.

His, he thought, and raised his eyebrow.

She bunched it up, put the material to her nose for a few seconds and sniffed. "What can I say? It's super soft and smells like you."

And on that note, she gathered all her things and strode across the room, disappearing into the bathroom and closing the door behind her.

★   ★   ★

DURING HER BATH, Raven pushed Lance and the unknown future aside. Instead, she closed her eyes and thought about Remy. Although he didn't know it, she'd heard him and Dex talking. Her name had stopped her from joining them and though she hadn't meant to eavesdrop… she had, while waiting for a good time to walk in and intrude.

When Dex had said goodbye, she'd rushed around the corner and let him go to his room without seeing her. She had every intention of telling Remy what happened, but she'd needed time to think and now she had it.

Married. Remington Sterling had been married. How had she not known that and why had he never mentioned it? An even bigger question floated around her brain. Was Raven just his woman of the moment as Dex had insinuated?

It shouldn't matter because she couldn't commit to anything without risking not just Remy—because she knew he could handle himself—but the people he loved. His sister and brothers. Lance would use anyone to get to her. It shouldn't matter, she thought again. But it did. Despite the obstacle keeping her from a happy future, she wanted to know she was special to him. Yes, he'd said as much to Dex but she wanted to hear him tell her himself.

She'd found a new loofah sponge in the linen closet in the bathroom and now she used it to coat her skin with the bubbles around her. The bathwater smelled like lavender and when she stopped thinking so hard, it relaxed her. Soon she'd leaned back against the tub, a plastic pillow behind her head, closing her eyes and just letting herself be.

She wasn't sure how much time had passed when a knock intruded and Raven startled, realizing she'd fallen asleep in the tub.

"I'm coming in!" Remy called and opened the door. "Oh good. You're alive in here. I was beginning to worry."

Feeling her cheeks flush, she said, "I fell asleep." The bubbles had all but disappeared and the water was cool.

He stepped into the bathroom and her gaze traveled over his sexy body. He was naked but for a pair of black boxer briefs and his substantial erection tented the soft material. Immediately, her body softened and she became aware of the heaviness between her thighs.

He let out a groan. "Stop looking at me like that or you'll find yourself soaking wet on the bed and my cock deep inside you before you can even blink."

Her cheeks warmed at his words. "You promise?"

With an eye roll, he picked up the large, fluffy bath towel she'd laid out and held it open. Rising, she let the water sluice over her skin, doing her best not to give in to impulse to shake it off like a wet dog.

She took his extended hand and let him aid her, stepping out of the tub carefully so as not to slip on the flooring. Once he'd wrapped her in the bath sheet, he began to pat her with his hands, letting the towel absorb the water as he rubbed it against her skin.

She closed her eyes and enjoyed being pampered but her thoughts from earlier came back to her. "Remy?"

"What is it?" he asked in a gruff voice.

The tone let her know he was as aroused as her,

but she had more important things to concentrate on. "I heard you and Dex talking in the family room."

His hands stopped moving and she opened her eyes to meet his gaze. "How much did you hear?"

"Why didn't you ever mention you'd been married?" she asked. She'd met Remy a little over two years ago and only knew him as a fun man who enjoyed dating. She'd also never seen him in a serious relationship. And in all that time, his past with other women never came up.

"Why don't you come to bed and we'll talk?" he suggested, and she nodded.

He walked out of the bathroom, leaving her to finish drying off. She pulled on his T-shirt. The one she never planned on giving back.

A few minutes later, she joined him in bed and she sat cross-legged, facing him. She waited for him to speak.

"I'm not sure where to start," he said. "So much of my past is tied up in my mother's murder." A muscle ticked in his jaw and he didn't meet her gaze, proof this conversation wasn't easy for him. "I'd planned on going to business school and follow in my dad's footsteps but once Mom was killed, becoming a cop was the only way I could channel the helpless feelings I had."

"I understand," she murmured, her heart aching

for his pain.

He eyed her warily. "If you heard Dex and I talk about my ex, you must also have heard us discuss my penchant for ending up with women who needed me." His frown and the light red stain on his cheekbones told her the admission embarrassed him.

She inclined her head. "I did overhear that, too. I didn't listen on purpose, at least not at first, but when I realized you two should finish your conversation, I... couldn't walk away."

"I'm not angry with you. I get it. And I wouldn't say I was hiding my past. I just don't think about it anymore." He lifted one shoulder in a half-hearted shrug. "I married my ex a short time after we met. She was the victim of a mugging and she'd been stabbed, too."

Raven's hand came to her mouth. "I'm sorry." She lowered her arm, twisting her hands together in her lap.

"She needed me and I guess I liked being needed."

Raven stiffened because this was the hard part. "Is that why we're together?" she asked, recalling Dex said something similar. "Like Dex said, my past was a mystery to you. Then my place was broken into. Now you're keeping me safe, and that's what drives you, right? Keeping women safe?"

He shook his head, his lips lifting in a grin. "You

know better. You must have heard me tell Dex you're different, and you are. In every way." His hands slid over hers and held on tight but instead of feeling better, the sad truth of her life intruded and though she'd initiated this conversation, it had gotten too deep.

"It doesn't matter." She pulled her hands out of his. "I'm never going to be free of Lance. I know it and so do you. He and Cassandra will do whatever they have to in order to keep him out of jail and he'll never give up on his obsession with me."

She lifted a pillow and pulled it into her lap, pressing it against the pain in her stomach. Because no matter how Remy felt about her, she couldn't let herself go and admit to feeling the same way. Because if this situation with Lance went on much longer, she'd have no choice but to run. To go somewhere he couldn't find her.

"I shouldn't have asked you about your marriage. It has nothing to do with me." She placed the pillow back in its spot and lay down, facing away from him.

He didn't reply but she heard the bedsheets rustle and soon he lay behind her and pulled her into his arms. He didn't say a word but she settled in the comfort and safety of his arms, and was able to relax.

REMY UNDERSTOOD MORE about Raven's fear than she knew. He also didn't believe his past had nothing to do with her. She'd overheard him talking about Sadie and his marriage and the notion bothered her enough for her to ask.

He hadn't been hiding the truth from her. He'd just pushed it into a part of his brain where old things piled up, rarely to be thought of again. He'd moved on from his ex-wife. He'd never get past his mother's murder. It had altered the course of his future.

Once he'd laid eyes on Raven, she'd pulled him in. She was who he was meant to be with. Until she was free from the stress and fear of who her brother would go after next in order to hurt her, Remy wouldn't push her for anything more than she was willing to give.

The next morning, he'd woken her up like any other morning they'd been together. He'd rolled her onto her back and hovered over her, treating her to a long kiss as he slid into her. Once they'd forgotten protection, they'd come to a silent but mutual agreement none was needed after that.

Now, at nine-thirty a.m., they were in the kitchen for breakfast. True to his word, Dex's suitcases were gone and so was he. Not only did his father have a groundskeeper on premises, he had a housekeeper, and since Dex had obviously let her know he was coming, the fridge was stocked with food.

Working together, Remy and Raven cooked breakfast, making two omelets and whole-wheat toast. For two people who'd never cooked as a team, they'd done pretty well.

While she finished at the stove, he placed orange juice and the coffee he'd made on the table. Once she sat down, he already knew the direction he planned to take the conversation. He was keeping things light.

"So, did I ever tell you how I made my fortune?" he asked.

She sputtered, having just taken a sip of juice. "I just assumed you had family money. I mean, I knew it wasn't from being a New York City police officer."

He lifted his mug for a drink of coffee. "There is that. We all have trust funds. But when I met Zach in college, he was determined to find Hadley. We now know she was in WitSec but all Zach knew was that she and her family had disappeared. We bonded over our hacking skills and I tried to help him dig into databases where we didn't belong."

Her pretty eyes opened wide. "What happened?"

"We got caught." He ignored his omelet in favor of storytelling. "But we got lucky, too. The feds were so impressed with our skills, they hired us to find holes in their databases and programs. Through our work, we met influential people in Silicon Valley. Zach and I developed our own anti-hacking software and sold it for enough to make us millionaires."

She grinned. "You're pretty impressive, Remington Sterling."

Chuckling, he said, "I'm glad you think so." Was he smug about it? Hell, yes. He and Zach had done it on their own.

She shook her head, eyes twinkling. They finished their food and cleaned up in easy silence and occasional small talk.

No sooner had they cleaned up breakfast than Raven's phone buzzed with a call. She answered immediately. "Hi, Caleb," she said, quiet when her brother was obviously talking to her. "He *what*?"

Her voice rose and Remy came up by her side, waiting as she finished the conversation, his curiosity and concern rising with every word Raven said.

"I'll get back to you with our plan. Love you," she said and disconnected the call.

"What's wrong?" Remy asked.

Her hands shook and he wrapped an arm around her and guided her to the family room where they sat down. Going with his gut, Remy pulled her into his lap. "Now tell me what happened."

"Lance tried to take Owen out of preschool."

Remy's blood froze, his skin prickling with the awareness that Lance had a plan they'd never considered. "He didn't succeed, right?" Though she'd said the word *tried*, Remy needed to hear it again.

"No," she said with a shake of her head. "The preschool knows who's on the pickup list. Lance couldn't have thought the teachers would believe he was Caleb. They aren't identical twins. I just don't get his thinking."

Remy slid his hand up the back of her shirt and rubbed her soft skin in a soothing, up-and-down motion. "I don't think he ever planned to get his hands on Owen. He wanted to shake you both up and he succeeded. You now know he's unpredictable."

"He told Caleb that he was just playing a joke on him. That he hadn't bothered with him since he's been out and he wanted to get his attention," she said.

"I call bullshit." That sick bastard was toying with both of his siblings but Remy had no doubt Lance's real target was Raven.

She shivered and Remy pulled her close, his brain spinning with the need for that bastard to violate his parole and land back in prison.

"Remy? I want to go home," Raven said. "And I need to see Caleb. We have to talk."

He knew better than to argue with her. She was emotionally distraught and he had no intention of making things worse. But he was equally curious and disturbed by her words. "Talk about what?"

"How to get rid of Lance once and for all."

Knowing she didn't mean that the way it sounded because she wasn't a killer, he managed a nod. "Go pack. I'll be up to help you in a few minutes."

Once she'd left the room, Remy picked up his phone and called Zach. No one was going to make any crazy plans without their approval.

Chapter Fifteen

B ACK AT REMY'S apartment in New York, Raven paced the floor in the family room, pausing to stare out the windows overlooking the city. It had snowed lightly overnight, the powder dusting the few green spaces she could see. She wished she'd had time to enjoy the grounds of the Sterling family compound, take a long walk outside in the frigid air, with Remy by her side. But of course, Lance had ruined that for her, too.

She didn't know how much longer she could live with her psycho brother's schemes. Especially without knowing his end game. She had good reason to fear him, Raven thought, recalling how she'd found Emily, battered and bruised. But she had better reason to stand her ground and get her life back.

The elevator into the apartment opened and she heard voices. Turning, she saw Caleb walk toward her, followed by Zach who was already in deep conversation with Remy.

"Caleb!" She ran to her brother and hugged him tight. "Is Owen okay? Where is he? He's safe, right?" If her adorable nephew was the least bit shaken up she'd throttle Lance.

"He's fine and he's in class," Caleb said, slinging an arm around her shoulder and leading her to the sofa. "He doesn't know anything happened. Lance spoke to someone at the school's front office and they turned him away, threatening to call the police if he didn't leave. The school called me immediately."

She nodded, letting out a long breath filled with relief. "Okay, good." She turned to Zach. "Hi. I didn't realize you were coming over today?" She said it more as a question than a statement.

He shot Remy a curious glance and waited for him to reply.

"Because the four of us should talk," Remy said.

"Why?" she asked, feeling defensive because he hadn't included her in his thought process. This whole situation was about *her*.

Remy ran a hand through his hair. "Because this mess can't go on. He's ruining your life."

She'd been thinking the same thing. "Well, next time I'd appreciate it if you'd include me in whatever you're planning that involves me."

He inclined his head in acquiescence. "Why don't we all sit down?" He gestured to the family room.

She led the way across the apartment and lowered herself onto a couch cushion. Caleb took the seat beside her, Remy and Zach across from them in the oversized club chairs.

"Where do we begin?" Caleb asked.

Remy's gaze fell to Raven. "Tell us what you're thinking, because you tossed and turned all night."

Yes, she had.

She immediately saw how this would go. Zach would be in charge because Remy assumed she'd cave faster if he, too, was against her idea. She had a feeling Remy knew exactly what she wanted to do, so she cut to the chase.

"I want to use myself as bait to draw Lance out. Though I hate playing games with a sociopath, and I'm aware it's a risk, we all know Lance won't be able to resist if he sees me alone."

"No!" Remy exploded, in a tone indicating he wouldn't give in. He pounded his hand on the arm of the chair for emphasis.

"I'm with Remy." Caleb folded his arms across his chest and shook his head at her, using his disappointed big brother look she'd seen often growing up.

"Tell me more," Zach said, his gaze on hers.

Remy's eyes opened wide. "You son of a bitch. If I thought you'd take her side, I wouldn't have asked you to come."

"Relax," Zach said. "I'm here to help you all end this mess. I want to know what Raven has in mind."

Doing her best not to smirk at Zach's acknowledgment she might have a valid idea, she spoke. "All we need to do is allow me to go back to living my normal life." She held up a hand before Remy could argue, which from his opened mouth, he intended to do.

"I'll still stay here," she said, doing her best to give him reasons to understand why she'd be safe. "You can watch me at all times. Put cameras up outside the bar, I don't care. Just let me do everyday things like taking out the trash from the bar, have my coffee break in the back alley, go to poetry slam, and let it *seem* like I'm alone. Give Lance the opportunity to come after me."

"I don't like it," Remy muttered.

"What happens when he grabs you?" Caleb asked. "What then?"

She shook her head. "Isn't anyone paying attention? Remy will be watching me from the bar or you can hire one of the bodyguards you mentioned who can blend in with the crowd. Lance won't realize I'm being protected."

"If he lays a hand on you, I'm going to kill him."

She rose and walked over to where he sat and knelt down, putting her hand over his. "We need him to violate his parole without it seeming like he was set up. But you'll be there to make sure nothing serious happens. A violation gets him back behind bars for the duration of his sentence. I just wish he could be put away for a lot longer."

Caleb cleared his throat.

Uncomfortable in her kneeling position, she stood and glanced at her brother. "What is it?"

"What I didn't mention yet was that after I took Owen to school this morning, I drove to Mom's to talk to my brother." Caleb rubbed his hands together in a nervous gesture. "I hate this because he's my twin. But... I think he's on drugs."

Remy leaned forward. "Why do you say that?"

"Because his eyes were like pinpricks, and he was antsy, and unable to remain sitting or standing in one place," Caleb said.

Silence followed his statement. Raven caught Remy and Zach exchanging glances. "What is it?" she asked. "No silent mental telepathy, you two." She pointed back and forth between them.

Zach rose to his feet. "It's just that if Lance is on drugs, *and* he's caught carrying, *and* if he's on hard-core drugs like meth or blow... he'll get himself slammed with a longer sentence. It's even better if he's carrying a weapon at the time."

She winced at the thought of Lance with a gun.

Remy nodded. "With his record, that's another return-to-jail card. But it's not like we can set him up to make it happen. He'd need to be playing fast and loose and be totally out of control."

"It wouldn't shock me if any of those things were true," Caleb muttered, head in his hands.

Raven felt sorry for her brother and wished she knew how to help him but she didn't even know how to help herself.

"I say we take some time to think," Zach said. "We can regroup soon and see if you can live with Raven's idea." He glanced from Caleb to Remy. "Because making her seem available to Lance is the best way to draw him out."

"I can do this," she assured them, not wanting them to think she'd cave out of fear.

Even if just the thought of Lance spiraling on drugs and carrying a gun scared her to death, there was no way she'd give up on her plan. She needed to do draw him out if she wanted to regain her life.

REMY LET HIS guests out of the apartment, knowing he and Raven needed to talk. He strode back to the family room but she wasn't there. He found her in the bedroom, sitting on the bed, a lost, dazed look on her face.

"Raven?" She jumped at the sound of her name.

"I didn't mean to scare you."

She nodded. "I know. Come here?" She patted the space on the mattress beside her and he slid onto the bed, joining her.

"What's up?" he asked, not knowing where her mind was after that meeting. True, she'd reiterated her desire to play a target but he wasn't sure she'd thought things through.

"I need you to trust me," she said. "There is no way I can even think about having a future unless Lance is gone. I want to see my nephew and not worry that Lance will devolve to the point where he'd hurt a child. Don't I deserve to be able to go out and have drinks with a girlfriend like Stevie without worrying she'll end up like Emily?"

"You deserve all those things and more but I don't want to lose the woman I love like I lost my mother!" His shout came as much of a surprise to him as it did to Raven, who'd jerked at his tone.

He blew out a calming breath. "I'm sorry. I didn't mean to yell at you."

She crossed her hands over her stomach and blinked back tears. "I know. Just like I know I want to say it back to you, but I can't."

His heart stopped beating in his chest. He'd been more aware of nearly losing control than he had of the words he'd been holding in for so long. He knew damn well she wasn't ready to hear the depth of his feelings and he'd never meant for them to come out.

"I know." He grasped her hands in his. "Forget I said it. I understand where your head is at. We can table all relationship conversations," he said, hoping he didn't regret not pushing her now.

"Remy, if I can't lure him out, I have to leave, and if I go, I won't tell *anyone* where I end up." A lone tear dropped down her cheek and he brushed it away with his knuckle.

He shook his head, ignoring the jolt of panic racing through him at the possibility of her disappearing forever.

"You're not going anywhere." He clasped her hands tighter. "I'll give your plan some thought and I'll talk to Zach and even Garrett." He hadn't invited the detective over today because his old friend had rules to follow that Remy didn't.

But when it came to putting any plan into action, he and Zach would figure out how to protect everyone by including the NYPD. The goal was to have Lance arrested and put away for a long time.

"Thank you." She threw her arms around him and crawled into his lap. "I'll be careful and I won't let him take me to a second location."

Pulling his head back, he met her gaze and caught her amused grin.

"Watching those true crime shows again?" He'd

caught her up at night in the family room watching TV when she couldn't sleep.

But she'd always end up back in bed with him come morning. And that was how he wanted things to remain. Which meant he'd give in to her plan. He'd have to trust her and the people he would strategically place around her to keep her safe. He had no other choice.

After coming to an understanding, they arrived at another one. She'd already called him out on telepathy with Zach but he and Raven also knew how to read each other's mind. In tandem, they rose from the bed to strip off their clothes. Once they were naked, she returned to her position on his lap but this time, she'd raised herself over him.

His cock stood at attention and she easily dropped down, coating him in her wet heat and taking him deep. And despite the fact that she wouldn't say the words back to him, he knew it was out of fear. Fear that she'd have to run.

And it was that fear inside him now that had him arching his pelvis and fucking up into her as she rocked her body, her clit rubbing against his pubic bone. They were both needy and desperate and it wasn't long before she stiffened.

"Oh," she moaned, the heady sound reverberating in his ear. "I'm coming so hard." She trembled and shook, grinding her pelvis into him as her pussy clasped his dick over and over.

Once she'd begun to relax, he knew her orgasm had finished and he leaned back on his hands and lifted his hips until he came, feeling his come spurt inside her.

A while later, they'd showered and collapsed into bed. No more words were spoken about Lance or love but as he held her, Remy knew that was exactly what they both felt.

The next morning, they were both ready for work, about to head downstairs to his SUV, when his phone rang.

Raven paused in front of the elevator, waiting for him to take the call.

He checked the screen and saw Dex's name. "Hello?"

"Rem, you need to get to Glen Cove Hospital. Dad's been admitted. They think he had a heart attack."

His own heart squeezed in his chest. "I'll be there as soon as I can." He disconnected and shoved his phone into his back pants pocket.

"What is it?" Raven asked.

"My father had a heart attack. I need to get to the hospital."

Her eyes opened wide, concern obvious as her

gaze softened. "I want to come with you. Is it okay if I get Stevie to cover?"

He immediately nodded, grateful for her presence. True, her coming along saved him from having to drop her off at the bar and make sure someone watched over her, but that wasn't the main reason.

Remy could not lose his dad and he definitely didn't want to find out how bad things were alone. He needed Raven and without asking, she wanted to be there.

Chapter Sixteen

REMY HATED HOSPITALS. The antiseptic smell reminded him of the night his mother died and the whole family had gathered in the waiting room for news. Shaking off that morbid thought, he held on to Raven's hand as they entered the ER waiting room where Dex had texted him to go.

"What happened?" he asked Aiden, since he was staying at their father's house.

"I…" He glanced from Lizzie to her daughter, Brooklyn, and Lizzie's face unexpectedly flushed.

"Your father was having dinner at the guesthouse. With me."

Remy raised his eyebrows, suddenly understanding the implication.

"We'd just finished dinner and he rose from his seat and put his hand to his chest. He couldn't breathe, he was dizzy and sweating." Her hands shook and Brooklyn stepped closer, wrapping an arm around her mom's waist. "I called 911 immediately," Lizzie said. "I didn't waste any time. I swear." Tears streamed down her cheeks.

"It's okay, Mom. Nobody blames you," Brooklyn

said, rubbing her mother's back.

Murmurs of agreement rose from his brothers and Fallon.

Remy glanced around at each of them, wondering what they knew about this newly revealed couple. They all shrugged or shook their heads and Remy didn't think any of them had been aware of Alex and Lizzie's relationship. The two had been good friends for years and Remy trusted that if anything romantic was occurring, eventually his dad would have let one of them know.

Until now, Alex Sterling hadn't been involved with a woman since his wife died. Not to Remy's knowledge, anyway. And if he and Lizzie just had been having a friendly dinner, she wouldn't have blushed so badly. Beyond that, his father's personal life wasn't something he wanted to consider.

He paced the stark waiting room. Raven had taken a seat, understanding that he needed time. He was just glad she was here.

Aiden and Dex walked over and Remy stopped their movement. "What do you know? What did they say when they brought Dad in?"

"Not a damn thing," Aiden muttered.

"They were more concerned with stabilizing him than reporting to the family." Dex put a brotherly arm on Aiden's shoulder.

Remy lifted a hand to run through his hair and realized he, too, was shaking. "Fuck."

"The Sterling family?" A female doctor in a white coat stood in the doorway.

"That's us," Remy said, stepping up and taking control. As the oldest, he felt it was up to him to hold it together for the rest of them. Dex seemed to be doing the same.

"Mr. Sterling had what we call a myocardial infarction. In other words, a heart attack."

Despite already thinking that was the case, Fallon gasped when the doctor confirmed the news. The redheaded doctor went on to explain about his father's heart not getting enough blood and how important fast treatment always was.

Behind him, Lizzie sniffed, and he knew she was worried she hadn't done enough to help. Nobody here would blame her and Remy hoped she knew that.

"Fortunately, the ambulance was called and arrived quickly. We were able to restore blood flow to the heart via a PCI procedure."

Even Remy's legs shook as he took in the news. "Will he be okay?" Dex asked.

The doctor nodded. "We want to run some tests and see if he needs any further treatment, so expect him to be here for a few more days."

"Thank you, Doctor." Remy extended his hand

and shook hers.

"You're welcome. You can go in and see him now. Two at a time," she instructed, then turned and walked back through the double doors.

"Please, can I go first?" Fallon asked, her eyes red-rimmed.

"Go ahead. Take Lizzie with you," Remy said. "I'm sure she needs to see for herself that he's okay."

The woman they all knew well gasped. "I couldn't do that. One of you boys should go with her."

Aiden strode over and held both her hands in his. "We all know who Dad will want to see. Go ahead."

"It's okay, Mom. I'll be waiting when you get back," Brooklyn said.

Lizzie smiled in gratitude. "I won't stay long. Come on, Fallon." Hand in hand, they walked back the way the doctor had gone.

Dex turned to his the rest of the group. "Who knew about Dad and Lizzie? Fallon? Brooklyn?" His tone sounded more like he was curious than upset.

They each shrugged.

Remy felt the same way. Maybe when he'd been younger, it might have bothered him to see his father moving on with someone new but Alex's focus had always been his kids. As far as Remy was concerned, his dad had been alone for too long.

They dispersed from their large group and he

found Raven sitting in a chair, waiting for him.

He strode over and sat down next to her. "I'm sorry I left you alone."

"I heard what the doctor said but I didn't want to intrude." Raven tucked a stray strand of hair behind her ear.

He frowned, taking her hand and pulling her closer. "You couldn't intrude if you wanted to. I need you here."

Her soft smile warmed him.

"Are you okay?" she asked, stroking his face in her hand.

"I'm not sure. I just know I'll feel better when I see Dad for myself."

"I don't blame you." She glanced up at him, her eyes wide with concern. "Why do I think you're going let everyone else go first?" she asked.

"Because you know I love my siblings?" She pursed her lips and he recognized that narrowed-eyed, *I'm thinking* face. "What?" he asked.

"Later," she murmured.

Why did he have a feeling he wasn't going to like what he heard?

IT HAD BEEN a long day, Raven thought, as she finally

changed into her nightshirt, otherwise known as her stolen T-shirt, and climbed into bed beside Remy. He lay with one arm behind his head, looking scrumptious with the sheet rumpled at his waist, his abdominal muscles on full display.

But tonight wasn't about sex. It was about talk and comfort, which she'd sensed Remy needed ever since getting the phone call about his father this morning.

She lifted the covers and crawled beneath. "Are you okay?" He'd been quiet since he'd gone in to visit his dad.

"Yeah. I'm just beat."

She nodded. "Did you talk to your father or did you just sit with him?" she asked, turning to face him.

"Dad was worn out. I just sat by the bed and let him know I was there."

Of course, she thought. Because after Fallon and Lizzie returned from their brief check, Aiden and Brooklyn had gone in to see Alex. There were many times today when Raven had gotten the sense there was something more than friendship going on between the two. Next was Dex and Jared, leaving Remy to go last, just as she'd predicted, and Alex, exhausted.

"You're a good brother, letting everyone else go first to see your father."

"I'm the oldest. I try and hold things together when shit goes bad," he said, surprising her.

She tipped her head to the side. "Does shit go bad often? Or are you talking about after your mom died?" She knew she was pushing him but she sensed he needed to release the hurt, pain, and guilt resulting from his choices that night.

"She didn't die, she was murdered," he muttered.

Oh, he was in a mood and she was right. He blamed himself for deciding to go out with a girl instead of having dinner with his mother. And now he felt like his siblings should take precedence in visiting with their dad because guilt was a bitch, as she knew from Emily's attack and her own resulting remorse.

She repositioned herself, curling her legs beneath her. "Remy." She placed a hand on his shoulder. "Your rational self knows it's not your fault. In the course of all your cases, how many people have you told the same thing?"

"Too many. And why are you psychoanalyzing me?" He pushed himself further back against the pillows and headboard.

"Because I think you'll feel better after you get this poison out of your system. I also think nobody in the family realizes how deeply you still blame yourself. Let me ask you something. Do you think your father blames you?"

He gritted his teeth. "I don't want to talk about this."

She leaned up on her knees. "But we're going to. Because you're the best man I've ever met and I hate to see you punish yourself."

He threw the covers off his waist and rose to his feet, grabbing for a pair of track pants that lay over the recliner.

"You can't run from your problems, Remy."

"Why the fuck not? You plan to," he said as he put his second leg into the pants and settled them on his hips before walking out the door.

She blinked, her eyes filling with tears. He'd turned his anger and frustration on her and it hurt.

AN HOUR AFTER he'd stormed out of the bedroom after having a tantrum like a child, Remy stared at the screen on the computer in his office. He was unable to focus on anything and hadn't accomplished one damn thing.

All he'd done was try to avoid the truth that Raven had hit on with accuracy. His guilt impacted his choices today. Oh, even without the remorse he felt for the night his mother died, he might have stepped back and allowed his siblings to go see his father first anyway. But he wouldn't have had the pain in his chest and the fear that he was to blame.

Why had this come up now, though? Today should have been about his father's health. When he let himself think about it, the answer was clear. If his dad died, they would have lost both parents and Remy felt he was to blame. He shook his head and groaned. No wonder he'd understood Lizzie's feelings so well. But if she wasn't at fault for her actions after his father's heart attack, if she'd done the best she could, was he at fault for being a kid?

Damn. Maybe he should have listened to the therapist his father had forced all the kids to see during their grieving period for their mom. Instead, he'd sat mulishly silent, until the man had told Alex he was paying for nothing and he didn't think he'd reach Remy at all. When his father asked Remy if he wanted to try another psychologist, he'd shaken his head. And that had been that.

Raven was smarter than he was, figuring him out in no time. And he'd treated her like shit.

"Dammit." Knowing he needed to apologize, he pushed his chair back and rose to his feet. He started to walk out of his office only to run into Raven. She still wore his T-shirt, which he had to admit he found fucking hot. But he didn't feel the same way about her red-rimmed eyes or the tear tracks on her pale skin.

She folded her arms across her chest and stared at him, chin tilted up, her eyes filled with hurt he'd caused.

He forced himself to meet her gaze. "I'm sorry. I was angry and I hated the fact that you were right so I lashed out. What I said was wrong, and cruel."

"Arguing is one thing but I don't fight dirty," she said, her voice hoarse. "If I wasn't worried about Lance, I would have been out of here for good. I had enough verbal slaps growing up. I won't take them from you."

God, he admired her strength and how she protected herself from anything that came at her. He was disgusted that she felt she had to do it from him.

"It won't happen again," he said, holding out his arms. He'd be more self-aware, even if dealing with his feelings felt like he was drowning in them.

She narrowed her gaze. "And you'll talk to your father and cleanse that guilt?"

The woman drove a hard bargain but since he'd planned on doing that anyway, and he'd have agreed to walk across hot coals if it meant she forgave him, he nodded. "I will."

A second later, she'd stepped forward and then she was in his embrace, letting him hug her to him and whisper words he *knew* she didn't want to hear.

His girl had her own issues when it came to dealing with feelings but he understood why. Her situation wasn't over and done with. He couldn't just demand she get over it or ask her to talk things through and move on. But no matter how difficult her world got, she didn't lash out at him.

He knelt and slid one hand beneath her knees, lifting her into his arms and heading for the bedroom where he held her for the rest of the night.

RAVEN STOOD IN front of the bathroom mirror. She splashed cold water on her face and patted her skin dry. As she went through her morning routine, her thoughts drifted to last night and how easily she'd forgiven Remy. Not just for his raised words but for storming out on her in the middle of an argument.

The only reason she had was because when she'd walked into his office to have it out with him, he'd been on his feet and ready to come back to bed. And because he'd apologized in seconds, which told her he'd been mulling over their argument just as she had. And since he'd obviously felt bad.

She wasn't one of those women who fell at a man's feet or was desperate to believe easy words but who knew he'd be repeating the pattern soon. No, Remy was a good guy who'd been in terrible emotional pain, so she pushed last night's events aside and moved on.

With that settled, his *other* words came back to her.

Another woman I love.

Remy loved her. If not for the argument after, she'd have been reeling from that revelation. Had she allowed herself to consider their connection, she'd have already known how he felt. He showed her every single day that he wasn't just in this for the *benefits*, she thought, her lips lifting in amusement. And no matter what she told herself, neither was she.

She loved the man who was protecting and caring for her. And under any other circumstances, she'd have wrapped her arms around his neck, looked into those sexy eyes, and said it back. Another thing she could blame Lance for. Taking away her ability to admit to loving the best man she knew.

Her smile turned into a frown. No thinking about Lance. Today was about being there for Remy.

When she walked out of the bathroom, he wasn't in the room so she dressed and went to find him, discovering him in the kitchen. She joined him and he handed her a bagel with cream cheese.

"For the road," he said. "I'm hoping to get to the hospital in time to be the first to see Dad."

She smiled at that. "Good. And if anyone else is waiting, just tell them you need a few minutes with him alone," she said and took a bite of her bagel, enjoying the delicious doughy breakfast. "After you talk to him, can we spend the afternoon at the bar? I am so behind on paperwork."

"I already asked Stevie to drop the laptop off along with the papers on your desk. I figured you could do your work here?"

Raven sighed. "Okay, Mr. Obvious."

"What does that mean?"

She shrugged. "Just that I can see through your *I'm just being so accommodating* act. You want me here and not at the bar where Lance just might show his face."

"Busted," he said, not the least bit bothered by being caught. "Come on. Just humor me until we have some kind of plan in place."

She stared at him for a good thirty seconds, hoping to convey her annoyance. But in the end, she knew why he was keeping her prisoner here and gave in. "Fine. But we're going to talk to Caleb and Zach again. Soon."

The worry lines she'd seen last night were back in his forehead as he agreed with a nod.

Chapter Seventeen

W HEN THEY ARRIVED at the hospital, Remy was relieved to see Dex checking in at the main desk, too. On the drive over, he realized he couldn't leave Raven alone in the waiting room. He'd been racking his brain, trying to figure out a solution for where she could sit while he talked to his father. Now he had one.

Dex waited as Remy gave his name and received a pass to stick on his shirt, along with a reminder that it was two people allowed up at one time.

They walked over to the chairs in the lobby and Remy turned to his brother. "Can you stay here with Raven while I go see Dad? I need to talk to him and I don't want to leave her alone." Worst case, he'd have brought her into the room with him but he'd prefer privacy to have this heart-to-heart with his dad.

"Of course. I can get to know her better."

Remy glanced at Raven. "Are you good?"

She smiled. "I think I can handle hanging out with the hottest quarterback in the league."

"Retired hottest quarterback," Dex said with a smug grin.

Remy shook his head at his brother's ego. "I notice you aren't arguing about the word *hottest*."

"What can I say? When you've got it, you know it."

After rolling his eyes, Remy turned to Raven again, raising his eyebrows. "And you? Flirting with my brother in front of me?" He kept his tone light because he was joking.

"I'm just repeating what I read about him on social media!" she exclaimed. "We all know *you're* the hottest Sterling brother," she assured Remy, obviously stroking his ego, and he liked it.

"Hey! I take offense to that," Dex said.

Remy slapped his brother on the side of the head. "Take care of my girl. I'll be back soon."

With a sudden twist of nerves in his gut, he walked away from Raven and Dex, and toward the elevator, heading to visit his father.

He arrived at his dad's room just as a nurse walked out along with an orderly who stepped over to the food cart, then moved on to the next room.

The nurse paused. "Are you here to see Mr. Sterling?"

Remy nodded. "I'm his son."

The young woman smiled. "I assumed as much. He told me he has four of them. Go on in. He's eating breakfast."

"Thanks." Remy knocked once and walked in.

His father sat up in bed, the table turned so he had a tray in front of him. "Remy!" Alex sounded happy to see him.

"Hi, Dad." He took in his father's coloring, which was much better than it had been yesterday, his pallor no longer pasty and white. "You're looking well."

"I feel better. The doctors want to run some tests so I'm here for another couple of days. They want to monitor me."

Remy nodded, relieved the hospital wasn't just releasing him. "That's good. I'll feel better with more answers. This way you'll know how to take care of yourself."

"They say I have to give up red meat, among other things." His dad grimaced. "They're even sending a nutritionist in to talk to me. Lizzie wants to be here to make sure she can follow the diet they prescribe."

Remy was grateful his father would have someone to monitor his meals and behavior, at least in the beginning until he got used to a new routine. That thought reminded him of his mom, who wasn't here to keep tabs on his dad and the reason Remy wanted to talk.

As his father ate his oatmeal, Remy pulled up a chair and settled in by Alex's bedside. "So... you and Lizzie?" He brought up the easier conversation first.

Alex put down the spoon. His cheeks flushed as he

met Remy's gaze. "We discussed how to tell you kids but she wanted to wait. And I... I'm worried about how you'd all take the news. Especially Fallon. She has the softest heart." His dad put a hand over the organ in his chest that was causing him issues.

Remy clasped his hands together, resting them on the side of the bed. He drew a deep breath before diving in. "First off, none of us have spoken about things since yesterday but I don't have an issue with you two as a couple." It wasn't easy to discuss his father's personal life and Remy did his best not to squirm in his chair.

"I appreciate it." Alex glanced down but his cheeks were still flushed red, telling Remy this talk wasn't any easier for him.

"If anything, I'm happy to know you have someone who cares about you and it was obvious to me, even before yesterday, that Lizzie does. She's been good to us all."

His father nodded. "But she's not your mother."

And wasn't that the crux of it all? "No. And I know we rarely talked about that night... mostly because I clammed up and refused."

"Son, I wish you'd opened up to someone. To me, the therapist I spent a fortune on for all of you kids, or at least to each other. I hated seeing you in such emotional pain. Still do." His father's voice grew raspy.

Remy understood. He had a lump in his throat the size of Texas and couldn't find a way to speak over it. But he'd come here for a reason and he swallowed hard. "It's my fault."

He glanced up to find his father narrowing his gaze. "What is?"

"Mom's murder. If I had gone out for dinner with her as planned, she'd wouldn't have been home when that bastard broke in." The words poured from his soul. Words Remy had buried that night and pushed down deeper every year since.

"Dammit!" His father raised his voice and the monitor began to flash.

Remy jumped up from his seat. "Calm down before I kill you, too."

His father took a deep breath and relaxed his breathing for a long, interminable minute. The lines became less erratic on the monitor and nobody came in to yell at him for upsetting his parent.

"That's what you think? All these years, and *now* I find out you've been holding that bullshit inside you?" his father asked.

Remy knew Alex wasn't angry at him, he was upset with himself for not figuring out Remy's issues sooner. Not that he could have. On that subject, Remy had been a closed book.

"If anyone's to blame for your mom's death, it's

me," his dad said.

"But—" Remy tried to interrupt.

"No. I knew Mr. Peterson was unhinged after the losses he took in the market. I advised him against making those investments but he insisted I do it anyway. When I saw the stocks dropping, I called him and strongly recommended he pull out. Peterson refused and told me they'd rebound."

Remy lowered himself into his seat, knowing his dad wasn't finished talking.

Alex shook his head, his hands curled into fists on the hospital blanket. "If I'd listened to my gut, if I'd fired him as a client, if I'd refused to invest as he asked…"

"That's so wrong," Remy said, shocked at how his father felt. "You aren't responsible for another man's actions!"

"I know," Alex said softly. "And neither are you. You were a teenager who had the hots for a girl. Your mother called me after you left the house. Said she was glad you had a date." His father's wistful smile tugged at Remy's heart. "That was the last conversation we had, but your mom was happy for you."

The knowledge eased the pain and the heavy burden Remy had been carrying for so long. "And you don't blame me?" he asked.

His father shook his head. "No more than I blame

myself, though it took me years of therapy to accept that."

Remy's lips twisted, feeling wistful. "I wish I'd been less stubborn about it."

"You would have saved yourself a lot of pain," his dad said. "You should know though, I grieved your mom. Deeply." He dipped his head.

"I remember. We moved in with Grandma and Grandpa." His father's parents had taken good care of them when Alex couldn't do it all himself. Now they were on a cruise to Alaska, living their best later years, and they deserved it.

His father picked up the spoon, then placed it back in the bowl. "Damn slop," he muttered.

Remy laughed. "Better get used to it."

"Lizzie's a better cook than this. I'll be fine."

Remy rose from his chair. "I'm glad you have her, Dad."

"And she'll be glad you accept us."

He gave his father a brief hug, careful not to disturb the wires. "I'll give you a call later."

"Remington."

He startled at the name people in his life rarely used. His mom had discovered the old TV show, *Remington Steele*, and insisted on naming him after what she called, the dapper main character. He shook his head at the memory.

"What?" he asked his father.

"No more guilt. Your sister told me you're taking care of Raven?" His father knew her from his time visiting The Back Door.

Remy nodded, keeping the details to himself so as not to upset his father or cause him stress. "She's the one, Dad."

Alex smiled and looked like his usual self for the first time this morning. "Be smart and lock her down, then."

"I will," Remy laughed as he made the promise, leaving his father in a much better mood than he'd been when he'd arrived.

And he had Raven to thank for it.

RAVEN SENSED REMY'S better mood the moment he walked toward her after visiting his father. Even his step was lighter. She asked if their talk went well and his smile told her all she needed to know. Grateful he'd had a heavy burden lifted, she didn't press for details. It was none of her business and all that mattered was the end result.

Once they'd said their goodbyes to Dex, they returned to Remy's building, parking downstairs in the garage.

"Let's go to the lobby to pick up the laptop Stevie dropped off," he said, as they walked to the regular elevator and not the one leading to the penthouse.

In the lobby, they waited while another resident had a conversation with the man seated behind the desk and when he walked away, Remy stepped up.

"Hi, Harris. Did someone drop something off for me?" Remy asked the blond-haired man.

"Yes." He reached down and returned with the black laptop and a sheaf of papers held together by a rubber band, causing Raven to wince at the work that had piled up.

But at least it would keep her busy and take her thoughts off still being a prisoner in her own life.

"Thanks," Remy said, accepting the computer.

"One more thing," Harris said. "A gentleman left something for a guest of yours? Raven Walsh?"

Before she could panic, the man reached under the counter again and this time, he held a familiar-looking bakery bag in his hand.

Raven grinned. "God, I love my brother," she muttered and accepted the bag.

Chuckling, Remy thanked the doorman and together, they returned to his apartment where she headed straight for the kitchen. Once she'd stepped inside, she walked to the counter and opened the bag, just knowing Caleb had brought her donuts again.

"This is Caleb's way of calming me when I'm upset," she said to Remy. "Want one?"

"And give you one less donut to look forward to? No thanks. I'm going to run on the treadmill at the gym downstairs later today. Wouldn't make sense for me to eat that first."

She looked him over, taking her time, letting her gaze travel over the long-sleeve hunter green Henley he wore that clung to his muscles beneath. "So that's how you keep in shape."

"Treadmill and weights," he said. "And stop staring or I'll be the one eating a special treat and the donuts will have to wait."

She picked up the sexy innuendo and her pussy clenched with desire. He rarely had to do more than indicate he wanted her and she was ready for him. "Cut that out," she said, feeling the heat rise to her cheeks.

He grinned, then turned to take a plate out of the cabinet.

Opening the bag, she pulled out three donuts and placed them on the white dish. A piece of paper fell out. "I bet Caleb left me a note... or maybe Owen drew me a dinosaur," she said, opening the folded paper.

I hope you enjoy your favorite donuts as much as I'm enjoying our little game. You can hide but I'll always find you.

She read the familiar script and her stomach bottomed out, panic filling her. Nausea replaced her hunger and she dropped the note.

"What is it?" Remy asked, snatching up the paper. "That son of a bitch."

She wrapped her arms around herself and stepped back from the counter and the food she'd wanted so badly only seconds before. "Why won't he just leave me alone?"

Remy wrapped his arms around her and she felt safe. Safe in this tower in the sky and safe with him. But she couldn't become a hermit for the rest of her life.

After a few minutes of comforting her, Remy released her. He pulled out his phone and dialed a number. She didn't ask who he was calling. She was just so tired of living this way and nothing he did or said would change that.

"Garrett? Yeah, hey. Listen..." Remy went on to explain the things Lance had done, ending with the offending note. "I know it's not enough to get a TRO but can you take a ride out to Chappaqua and have a talk with the SOB? If I go myself I'll beat him to a bloody pulp and I'm useless to Raven behind bars."

She winced at his statement and shook her head

wildly. The last thing she wanted was a confrontation between Remy and Lance. Thank God he was thinking rationally and had asked the detective to go instead.

"I'll pack this gift up in a plastic bag for you to pick up," Remy went on. "Oh, and just Raven and I touched the note." A few more seconds of quiet passed where she assumed Garrett was speaking and then, "Thanks. I appreciate whatever you can do. Yeah. See you soon."

Remy disconnected the call and met her gaze. "I feel so fucking useless."

"And I just want this to be over. There's only one way to end this and you know it. Let me draw him out, Remy. You can make up the plan, name the people who will protect me, the officers who will grab him, whatever you and Garrett come up with. But let's be proactive." Goose bumps had risen on her arms beneath her long-sleeve shirt and she shivered.

He narrowed his gaze. "You're scared."

She blew out a long breath, opting for honesty. "I'd be stupid not to be afraid but I trust you to protect me. Now I need you to trust me to handle myself."

Silence followed. His brow furrowed and she could almost see the internal argument he was having with himself. She only hoped he'd come down on her side in the end.

Chapter Eighteen

A FEW DAYS had passed since Lance's gift ended up on Remy's doorstep. Every morning since, Remy and Raven stopped at the hospital for a visit with his father. One Remy pre-arranged with one of his male siblings so someone would sit with Raven in an upstairs waiting room. Remy didn't need her in the lobby, exposed to anyone walking in or out.

Today, his father was being discharged which allowed Remy to breathe easier and focus on what he wanted to do about Raven's request to be bait for Lance. Understanding that Remy had a full plate, worrying about his father, she'd given Remy space and hadn't pressured him for an answer. Now though, Alex would be home and Remy could free up his mental energy.

He'd invited his brothers to his apartment tonight, along with Garrett and Zach. They'd all arrived, knowing Remy wanted to discuss the Lance problem. Meanwhile, Raven was hanging out at Fallon's apartment, along with Stevie and an Alpha Security bodyguard watching over them. It was the only way Remy would allow a girls' night and he understood

Raven needed an escape from his apartment.

Now, with his apartment full, Remy filled the men in, and as he spoke, he realized he was tired of talking about Lance Kane and having his life dictated by the sick fuck. He could only imagine how Raven felt. Zach went next, reiterating why he thought Raven's idea of being bait had merit.

"I want this bastard behind bars again so Raven can live her life," Remy said.

Garrett leaned forward in his seat. "Then I agree with Zach," Garrett said. "Let her do that."

"Can you guarantee her safety if he shows up and tries to grab her before I can get to her?" Because Remy would be inside the bar, not right by her side. Not if they wanted to give Lance the opportunity to strike.

Garrett hesitated. "There's no way I'll be able to get anyone assigned to watch her," he said, making Remy's gut clench.

"So how can you ask him to put her in danger?" Aiden asked.

Though Remy hadn't been able to spend time with his wanderer sibling since he'd returned home, the twenty or so minutes the brothers had together before Garrett and Zach arrived had been enough time for Remy to lay out his feelings for Raven. The others might not be in a relationship but nobody gave him shit for it. Well, not too much. Just enough to know things were normal between them all.

"Because I have enough vacation time coming to watch over her myself," Garrett said.

Remy relaxed upon hearing that. Though he had faith in himself to look out for Raven, knowing Garrett was there helped him accept the inevitable decision.

"What do you think, Rem?" Jared asked, glancing his way. His brother loosened his tie. He'd come straight from work and was still wearing his suit.

Remy groaned. "I was going to keep fighting it… until that damned bakery drop-off and threatening note. Lance will keep escalating and Raven's right. It isn't fair that she has to keep watching over her shoulder, being afraid all the time."

"Remember, no setting him up," Garrett warned. "Either he fucks himself or we wait until he does."

Zach met Remy's gaze. The two had been friends long enough that they could read each other's thoughts. They each had been mulling over that very idea.

"I mean it, you two," Garrett said, obviously catching their interaction and assuming they were making separate plans.

Remy nodded, meaning it. "I might have considered it but I wouldn't jeopardize an arrest by making it anything but legit."

"Agreed." Remy's words and Zach's firm tone seemed to appease Garrett, who pushed himself to his feet. "Okay, I'll put in for vacation time and be in touch."

"I'll leave with him. My wife is home waiting." Zach and Hadley had come to their New York City apartment while this situation played out.

He rose and followed Garrett to the elevator.

Once the doors closed behind them, Remy glanced at his brothers. "You all understand, right? I have no choice. Hell, I'm worried if I don't Raven will take matters into her own hands and do it anyway." That or she'd run. Neither solution was an acceptable one.

"I can't imagine it's easy for you," Aiden said. "I know after Mom died, the thought of letting any woman I care about put herself in danger is scary as fuck."

Grateful that his brother understood, Remy nodded. "That's always on my mind."

"But Raven will have you, Garrett, and any one of us you need around to protect her," Dex said.

The others murmured in assent.

And that's why he loved his siblings. They might be a large family but they were also a tight unit. "As much as I appreciate that, you all have jobs to do."

"Speak for yourself," Aiden said. "I'm on leave."

"And I'm retired." Dex grinned. He rose and walked over to the bar. "Does anyone want a refill? There's another bottle of Dirty Dare Scotch when this runs out."

Remy kept his friend's family liquor stocked at home. In addition to owning the bars and the PI business with Remy, Zach had a stake in Dirty Dare Spirits, a company his brother, Asher, started and had his siblings invest in. The success rivaled Casamigos and other celebrity-owned brands. From what Zach said, Asher had been offered plenty of money to sell but so far, the company remained in the family's hands.

Dex filled everyone's glass and the evening turned into joking and ribbing like they'd always done growing up.

Remy left them talking and rose, walking over to the huge window he often caught Raven staring out of, taking in the city.

"You okay?" Dex asked, joining him. Because they were the same age and had been friends even before Dex's parents died and he came to live with the Sterlings, he and Dex shared a tight bond. Remy wasn't surprised he was the one who'd come to check on him.

Remy shrugged. "Unsure."

"Understandable." Dex put a hand on his shoulder. "Try to relax. I have faith everything will work out."

Remy attempted to feel the same way but the knots in his stomach had him on edge. "I think I'm going to head over to Fallon's."

"And interrupt girls' night?"

Remy grinned. "I don't think Raven will mind."

Dex rolled his eyes. "And you talk shit about *my* ego?"

"I can't wait to see the woman who knocks you off your feet."

"Not happening," Dex insisted. "There might have been someone… once. But it wasn't meant to be."

That came as a surprise and Remy narrowed his eyes. "Who? Because I'd remember if you ever mentioned someone."

"You probably would have, if I ever gave you her name." Dex finished his drink. "Come on. I'll help you kick the others out and you can get going."

Remy didn't care if they stayed to hang out but when he and Dex announced they were leaving, everyone else said they'd go home too. So Remy headed to pick up Raven from his sister's and hoped she wasn't too drunk to talk when they got home.

FALLON'S APARTMENT WAS as eclectic as the woman who owned it, decorated with bright colors and fun prints on the walls. Instead of a penthouse like Remy, Fallon lived in a loft in Tribeca.

When Fallon had invited Raven to hang out, she told Raven to bring a friend. Raven had no doubt either Remy had told his sister that she was a loner or Fallon had figured it out for herself. The woman wasn't just pretty and smart, she was intuitive, too.

"I love the art on the walls," Stevie said, pointing to a colorful print behind the plush white sofa where they were sitting on. A little girl was skipping rope and the only color was a bright burst of hot pink in a bow on her head.

Fallon beamed, her eyes glittering like golden gemstones, reminding her of her brother's gorgeous iris coloring. "Thank you. I created that one myself."

Raven raised an eyebrow. "What do you do for a living? Or is it a hobby?" she asked.

Fallon shook her head. "I do silk screen pop art prints and I own a gallery nearby."

"Oh, wow! I'd love to come see it sometime," Stevie said. "You're so talented!" She picked up her glass of cranberry juice and vodka and took a sip.

When they'd arrived and Fallon offered them drinks, all three wound up with the same choice. Then she led them to the white sofa. Raven and Stevie hesitated, not wanting to go near the no doubt expensive sofa and spill the berry-colored drink by mistake. Fallon had waved them off and informed them the couch was from Wayfair and even if it had been expensive, she wouldn't care. It was meant to be enjoyed.

Raven was still nervous and tended to drink often to make sure there wasn't much at the top of the glass. She'd wondered if she'd end up plastered by the time the night ended but soon after arriving, she'd realized Fallon just wanted to get to know her and she was touched that Remy's sister had made the effort.

As usual, she tried to ignore the twisting in her stomach that warned her being with these women put them in possible danger, assuming Lance somehow was following her and knew who she cared about. But Remy knew about the invitation before Fallon had extended it and he'd arranged for security so Raven could go. He somehow sensed Lance's grip on her life was becoming stifling so he'd figured out a way to let her have fun. He'd even promised to put a permanent guard on Fallon and Stevie afterward, and that had allowed Raven to agree to come.

How permanent the Alpha Security guard was remained to be seen. Remy was meeting with his detective friend tonight, along with Zach and his brothers. The brothers wanted to hang out and Remy planned to discuss her situation with the detective and Zach, both men he trusted.

When Zach's now wife had issues with her father's mob associates, she'd run to Zach for help. And he'd protected her, then put in motion something similar to what Raven suggested; drawing out the people who were making Hadley's life hell. Raven prayed they'd talk Remy into letting her do the same.

"Fallon, how's your father doing?" Stevie asked. "I know Remy took time off while he was in the hospital."

Fallon sighed. "He's home and feeling better. Thanks for asking. The doctors are optimistic since it was a mild heart attack. But he needs to take it easy for a while. My brother, Jared, works with him and now that Aiden's home, he's going to help out so Dad can stay home."

"What about you? Are you okay? I know Remy took his heart attack hard," Raven said.

Fallon drew a deep breath, remaining silent while she closed her eyes, obviously attempting to compose herself.

"I'm sorry. I didn't mean to upset you."

She waved a hand, dismissing Raven's concern. "It's fine. I'm... I guess you could say I'm a daddy's girl and proud of it. More so since Mom died. I was only ten and I clung to him afterward."

Thinking of her own parents and their deaths, a lump rose in Raven's throat. "Understandable," she murmured.

"But the doctors' prognosis helped me calm down." Fallon picked up the bottle of vodka and poured a touch more into her glass.

Stevie did too but Raven declined. She wanted to be clearheaded to hear what Remy and the guys discussed.

"So," Fallon said. "You and my brother, hmm? I like it." She tipped her glass back and took a sip.

"So do I," Stevie said, saving Raven from having to reply.

Which was good since she didn't feel like getting into the whole Lance problem or the potential that she might decide to pack up and leave. She was as over Lance as she was of her own thoughts about him.

"You should see Raven and Remy together." Stevie fanned herself and grinned.

Raven shook her head. "Cut it out," she muttered.

"What about you, Stevie? Any special guy in your life?" Fallon curled a leg beneath her and leaned back.

Her friend stuck out her lip in a pout. "No one." She lifted her glass. "But Raven's brother, Caleb, is super cute." She waggled her eyebrows and took a long drink.

"Oooh a potential match. I like that."

But Raven stiffened. "Unless Lance goes back to prison, you stay away from my brother," she warned Stevie. "I do not want to have to worry about you."

With a sigh, Stevie curled up into her corner of the couch. "I get it."

Dammit, Raven thought. Not only was she a party pooper but she was also the biggest worrier on the planet. And she was sick and tired of all of it.

"Okay, let's raise the mood," Fallon said, rising and walking over to where she'd left her phone on a counter.

She pressed a few buttons and soon music filled the large room. "One day, we'll all go out to a club and party and I'll introduce you to my friends but until we can, let's dance here!"

Fallon didn't stop until they humored her and before Raven knew it, they were spinning and laughing and she'd even finished two glasses of her drink.

By the time Remy arrived to bring her home, she fell into his arms, all thoughts of Lance buried where they should be.

Chapter Nineteen

RAVEN COULDN'T BELIEVE Remy had agreed to go along with her plan. He'd brought her home and because she was tipsy, he'd carried her out of the elevator and into bed. Next thing she knew, she was waking up the next morning with a nice little headache and a glass of water and two acetaminophens by the side of the bed.

She'd also found a note from Remy letting her know that he was at the gym, a security guard was outside the private elevator on the ground floor, and he'd be home in time for them to go to work. While he was gone, she showered and made herself a breakfast of scrambled eggs and hash browns, then holed up in Remy's room, reading a book on the Kindle app of her phone.

When he arrived home, he stopped by where she was curled in his recliner, and he paused to kiss her long and hard. "You might want to get ready for work. You got your wish. Operation Bait Lance begins today." And on the way to the bar, he'd laid out the details worked out between himself, Zach, and mostly Garrett. She owed the detective a huge thank you for taking his own personal time to help her out.

Once at work, Remy stuck to her like glue, as in, he didn't disappear into his office at all. No doubt he feared her going outside while he was unaware.

The one time Raven did take the garbage out back for the first time since Lance's release, her heart pounded hard in her chest. But she knew that Remy had worked fast, having cameras installed first thing this morning to watch the alley, and out front, as well. Money bought whatever you needed, whenever you needed it, something Raven had learned from the Kanes. But in this case, Remy was doing it to protect her and she was grateful.

Remy remained close by as she stepped outside into the fresh air alone, tossing the trash and stalling for a little while. She didn't know where security was located, just that there were eyes on her, which helped her stay calm. When there was no sign of Lance, Raven returned inside to find Remy waiting, jaw clenched, fists curled and every muscle in his body tight.

Another time, she walked a delivery person out the door, for no reason other than to see if her stalker brother lurked where there were more crowds. Unaware of the plan, Stevie joined her a minute later and they talked for a while before going back inside. Again, no Lance. And Remy sat at a table next to the window overlooking the sidewalk, his tension high.

Raven had no doubt Lance was around, either waiting and watching, or trying to make her nervous. Either way, he was doing a fine job by staying under the radar. But it had only been half a day. For all she knew, this could go on for a long while. She didn't know how she'd survive the anticipation but she would.

By the time the dinner crowd dispersed and they were into the evening happy hour, Remy remained on a barstool, driving the servers crazy, micromanaging the night.

Paul, their head bartender, pulled Raven aside. "What's going on with the boss? Why is he watching over us? Does he have trouble with our work?" he asked for all the servers, his brow furrowed in concern.

Raven shook her head and sighed. "Not at all. Everything's fine. Don't worry, I'll talk to him." Raven pushed aside the iPad and scheduling app she'd been working on and walked over to where Remy sat.

"Can we talk?" she asked.

He looked her over, as if reassuring himself she was fine. "Sure." He rose to his feet and she led him to his private office and closed the door behind him.

"What's wrong?"

"This can't go on, you sitting out front, watching

over everyone, questioning their work. They're worried and when employees are worried, they make mistakes. Drop dishes. Serve the wrong drink." All things that had happened today. Before he could reply, she told him to sit.

To her surprise, he listened, lowering himself into a chair in front of his desk. The seat didn't have arms.

She walked over and straddled him, sitting down on his thighs, her pussy settled over his hard cock.

"What are you doing?" he asked through gritted teeth.

"Trying to relax you before everyone who works for you walks out all at once." She rocked her hips and arousal wound its way through her veins.

He braced his hands on her hips and lifted her off him, setting her on her feet. "Not walking around like that all night. Save it until we get home." His eyes were dark with desire. "But point taken. I'm driving the staff insane. You tell me how to watch over you, then?"

The concern in his voice wrapped itself around her heart. It was something she always wanted to feel.

"How about this? I promise I won't leave the bar to do anything without letting you know first. I swear."

He nodded. "I'll accept that."

She sighed in relief. "There's another reason I

brought you in here."

He cocked an eyebrow. "Do tell."

Rising onto her toes, she wrapped her arms around his neck. "You didn't give me a chance to thank you for allowing this. I know it wouldn't happen if you shut down the idea. So thank you," she said and pressed her lips to his.

I love you, Remy Sterling, she thought, not saying the words out loud. She promised herself that once Lance was out of her life, those would be the first words she said to this special man.

ONE WEEK PASSED, then another. After the first seven days, Garrett went back to work, stopping in daily on his lunch hour so Raven could take trips to her favorite coffee shop and an old-fashioned bookstore that was still in existence. No sign of Lance. A rookie friend of Garrett's replaced him when he needed to work and on the nights Raven had poetry slam, he followed at a discreet distance. Not even Remy clocked his tail.

The longer this went on, the more frustrated both Remy and Raven became, to the point where they were snapping at one another instead of getting along.

Today, Remy gave an agitated Raven a wide berth.

He still kept an eye on her but didn't approach her. She hadn't gone outside yet and he wondered if being fed up would make her do something rash. What, he didn't know. Lance had mentioned enjoying their game and he was for sure playing one.

Remy just hoped it didn't turn dangerous.

He was sitting in his office when the bar phone rang. "Remy Sterling here."

"Mr. Sterling, this is Lieutenant Charles from the NYPD. A bomb threat has been called into your establishment. Although we can't insist you evacuate your patrons, we highly suggest you do so until our bomb squad arrives and gives you the all clear to return."

"On it," Remy said, rising as he spoke.

Dammit. There was no way to know if it had been Lance on the phone or a real problem. He had no choice but to err on the side of caution. He gathered as many employees as he could and instructed them to calmly ask people to leave until the building was clear.

He asked one of the barbacks to check the bathrooms, office area, and to keep an eye on the emergency exit, one also used by the staff, so no stragglers ended up causing trouble inside.

Soon the patrons were filing out the back door and being instructed to head to the front of the building. Despite the fear on some people's faces, and the eye rolls from those who never believed in fire alarms or any other kind of threat, the crowd was impressively well behaved. Trampling was always a potential problem and Remy was happy there were no assholes in the group.

He glanced around for Raven, who had been by his side when he talked to the staff, only to find her holding open the door.

Meeting her gaze, he narrowed his eyes and gestured for her to move away from the exit. Ignoring him, she grasped onto the arm of a pregnant woman whose friends had obviously ditched her to get themselves to safety. People definitely showed their true colors in an emergency.

Remy's gut screamed this episode had everything to do with Lance and that he'd finally made his move. But as the owner of the establishment and having a *suggestion* from the NYPD, or what appeared to be the NYPD, he was required to act accordingly and that meant being the last person out.

"Remy!" Stevie's voice had him turning around. She pointed to a woman who was sitting in a chair, head bent between her legs, clearly having a panic attack.

Shit. No way could he leave her. "Get outside and call 911, make sure they're sending an ambulance." He didn't want to take any chances. "I'll help our customer outside."

He spared another glance toward where he'd seen Raven earlier, but she was gone. His gut churned but he was unable to leave this panicked woman, whose breaths were coming way too fast, alone inside his place of business.

He knelt down to talk to her. "Miss? What's your name?"

"M… Melissa."

"Hi, Melissa. I'm Remy." As he went through the motions of talking to her and coaxing her to her feet, his thoughts were on Raven.

He had to hope the security guard he'd hired had an eye on her, that Garrett had heard about the bomb threat and was on his way over, and that this whole fiasco was a false alarm. Most of all, he prayed his hunch was wrong. That this had nothing to do with Raven's psychotic brother.

Unfortunately, Remy's track record was pretty damn good and there was every chance Lance was about to strike.

AS SOON AS Remy explained the phone call from the police, Raven got to work. As the manager, she needed to set a calm example for her employees and show them how to talk to the customers and escort them outside and to the front sidewalk in an orderly fashion.

She stood by the door, keeping an eye on the room and making sure everyone left. That's when she noticed a heavily pregnant woman holding her lower back as she made her way, alone, to the exit.

Raven rushed over to help her. "Are you okay?"

The pretty brunette shrugged. "My lower back has been bothering me all day but I also have sciatica with this pregnancy. So who knows what it is? It's my third." She blushed at the admission.

Raven winced, hoping it was back pain and not labor. "Well, let's get you out of here. Where are the women I saw you with earlier?" Raven asked.

The brunette frowned at the question. "They're work friends not friend friends, if you know what I mean. And I learned they won't ever fall into the latter category."

They made it to the door and walked out. Except for Stevie, the barback watching the emergency exit, and Remy who was taking care of a woman who looked ill, everyone was out. She wasn't worried about there being an actual explosive in the bar. Lance wouldn't involve the NYPD and she was sure it was some kind of crime to call in a fake bomb threat. She had no doubt they would all be outside soon.

While she watched for them, she stood with the

woman she'd helped, waiting for an ambulance. The sidewalk where they'd met up was crowded. To her surprise, instead of giving up and going home or to another restaurant, most of the patrons gathered and stayed, everyone talking, asking questions and mostly wanting to appease their morbid curiosity. She likened the people gathered to those who passed an accident on the highway and slowed down to watch, causing traffic on the other side of the highway.

An officer began to urge people to cross the street and move away from the building, or better yet, to disperse. Not many listened.

Two ambulances pulled up to the curb alongside the police cruisers, blocking traffic so they could park in front of the bar. The paramedics hopped out and took the pregnant woman inside one of the vehicles, leaving Raven to cross the street and try to look for Remy or the guard who he'd assigned to watch her.

With the growing crowd, she was being jostled and shoved. She wasn't comfortable so she backed away from the tight group of strangers, instead walking along the periphery and occasionally rising onto her tiptoes to scout out someone she knew, to no avail.

She sighed and leaned against the building, away from the bulk of gawkers. She didn't have her purse but she had her cell phone in her pocket and she pulled it out to call Remy. As she held it up to her face to open the screen, she got the feeling she'd had weeks ago, that someone was watching her.

She spun around, facing away from the gathered people, but didn't see anyone. Her heart pounded harder and again she searched for Remy or a familiar face.

"Raven."

At the sound of her name, relief that one of her coworkers had found her first filled her... Except it wasn't a friendly face she saw.

It was Lance.

Chapter Twenty

B EFORE RAVEN COULD blink, Lance clamped his hand around her wrist, causing her to drop her phone, as he pulled her around the corner, giving her no time to run. Instead, she opened her mouth to yell and he clamped a hand over her lips, squeezing her cheeks too tightly.

"Don't," he said in a harsh, brutal tone that sent chills down her spine. "You scream or make a scene and I promise you I will hunt down every friend you have and make them wish they'd never met you."

She wished she'd never met *him*.

He released his hold on her face and grabbed her forearm hard enough to leave a bruise, but not before moving his sport jacket and revealing a handgun tucked into his dark jeans. "Got it?" he asked.

She took the threat seriously and managed a curt nod. She was both relieved at how he could screw up his parole by carrying the weapon and afraid of what he might do with it.

The pain in her face lingered and tears filled her eyes. She was frustrated that after all their preparation, Lance had found her without her protection detail.

Then again, the area was mass chaos because of the bomb threat, which made her a much easier target. Something he'd no doubt planned because she was sure now that he'd made the call.

Luckily, Lance let the gun remain in his pants, not pulling it on her. She wondered if she grabbed the weapon, would she be able to fire at an actual human being? She had to believe that yes, she could… if her life depended on it.

"Let's go." Lance dragged her around the corner where they were hidden from view, and since she had no choice because of his threat, she followed.

With a rough grip on her arm, he leaned against the brick building and peeked out at the main street. His head darted from side to side in a jerky motion. His erratic movements worried her.

"We fucking need to get out of here," he muttered, turning toward her.

She looked into his normally vacant eyes and just as Caleb had said, his pupils were tiny pinpricks. Not good for her now but excellent if he had more drugs on him when he was caught. And he *would* be captured. She couldn't allow herself to think any other way.

But for now, they were alone and she had to consider how she could keep herself safe. She'd never allow him to take her to a secondary location where he could do God knew what to her. She took some comfort in the fact that Remy had access to the tracking app in her phone and though she'd dropped it, she was close by and she hoped he would find her before Lance moved them.

She thought about the changes she'd noticed in her so-called brother. Gone was the façade of the society boy. Though he still wore a sport jacket, the white dress shirt beneath was wrinkled and one too many buttons were open at the neck, as if he couldn't stand the choking feeling of the collar. In fact, he was sweating in the winter.

Once again, he peeked beyond the alley. "Still loaded with fucking people," he said to himself, running a hand through his hair in agitation. "Need to get away." That same irritation sounded in his stilted words.

"Why can't you leave me alone?" she asked, trying to divert his attention and stall him.

He faced her and his lips turned up in a sneer as he raked his gaze over her, openly leering. "We grew up in the same house and every damn day, you teased me with that body and those big tits. I knew you wanted me. Then you played hard to get, like every other bitch I know."

He truly was insane, she thought, and narrowed her eyes, the revulsion swirling in her stomach making her nauseous. "I'm your sister," she spat.

"Not by blood." He raised a shoulder in that arrogant way of his. "And I can't say it would bother me much if we *were* related. If I want something or someone, it's easy to reach out and take it."

Bile threatened but she had to keep him talking. Someone would come looking for her soon, she was sure of it. She just worried no one would think to look down an empty street when there was a crowd of people she could be mixed in with.

"But the main reason I won't give up until I have you is payback." Lance's threat jolted her out of her hopeful prayers. "*You* put me in that *fucking* hellhole," he said bitterly. "Your testimony. So much for being family, right, *Caroline*?"

She cringed at the name she despised. "You attacked Emily. Beat her badly and you were about to rape her when I walked in. Did you expect me to let that happen?" she hissed.

He still gripped her forearm and pressed his thumbs into her soft flesh, grinning his evil smirk, as he caused her more pain. Instead of giving him the satisfaction of a reaction, she bit the inside of her cheek until she tasted blood.

"Yes, *sister*, I did. Where's that asshole ex-detective who's always with you?"

She wasn't surprised Lance had figured out who

Remy was. Ignoring him, she didn't reply.

"No need to answer. I was brilliant with the bomb threat phone call. Got everyone all panicked and separated. And now I have you and you're mine." He leaned over and met her gaze, then to her disgust, he licked her cheek.

She gagged and jerked back, only serving to hurt herself when he refused to let go.

"Raven!?"

She stiffened as a familiar voice called out her name, his loud yell both welcome yet . . . not.

Lance wouldn't hesitate to shoot him. She knew it and would do everything she could to protect the man she loved.

"Answer and he's a dead man," Lance said in a low voice and patted his weapon for emphasis, confirming her greatest fear.

He was back to anxiously peering out to the street, then ducking back again, his movements jerky, his composure like a strung-out junkie.

Trying to tamp down her panic, Raven closed her eyes and envisioned her location. The building the bar was in was across the way on a main street where cars passed by all the time. Unless the police had closed it off by now due to the bomb scare. She'd heard someone yelling at the people to disperse and go home earlier, so maybe the area wasn't as crowded as it had been.

She didn't know, but she needed to run... *away* from the innocent people and far from Remy and anyone looking for her. If Lance shot at her, so be it. The cops would be on him in seconds and that mattered more than whether she was hit by a bullet. She'd rather save Remy from that fate.

She cringed at the thought of being hit by a bullet but gathered every ounce of strength and courage she had. "Lance?"

He turned toward her, his eyes wild and unfocused.

"I'll go with you if you leave Remy alone," she told him.

He studied her through narrowed eyes, gauging her honesty. He must not trust her because his features morphed into the angry man she'd seen hovering over her roommate, cheeks flushed, lips pinched, ready to cause pain.

"Lying bitch," he said, his anger turning him into a monster.

This was it. Time to act. She'd done reading on self-defense after he'd attacked Emily and Raven had been afraid Lance would get out and come after her. The solar plexus was the best place to aim in order to knock the wind out of someone.

Using her free arm, she pulled back and with her

palm struck straight into the soft spot beneath his ribs and above his stomach, aiming upward as she hit.

He groaned and doubled over and she took the opportunity to run out to the main street. Just as she screamed for help, Lance grabbed her ponytail and yanked so hard she saw stars. Her eyes teared, blurring her vision, and she tripped, falling hard onto her knees on the sidewalk.

"Get up, bitch." He pulled her up by her hair again and pressed his gun against her rib cage.

Feeling the dig of the weapon, she remained on her knees and prayed she'd pass out and not feel any pain when he pulled the trigger. No way would she go anywhere with him when he planned to rape her.

"Hey!" a large, bulky-shaped man yelled. "Let her go!" He shoved Lance so hard he released Raven, then stumbled… into the street and in the path of an ambulance pulling away from the curb.

Raven watched in horror as the vehicle slammed into Lance's body. She screamed as he went airborne for seconds before landing on the ground with a loud, dull *thud*.

He lay motionless, and she had no idea if he was dead or alive.

"Miss? Miss. Are you okay?" the man asked, but Raven couldn't answer.

She was too busy watching people, including

armed police officers, surround Lance. And Raven knew it was finally over.

AS THE OWNER of the bar, Remy exited last and immediately looked for Raven. He didn't see her anywhere near the back entrance or when he went around to the front of the building. The police and bomb squad arrived before Remy could take off and find her, forcing him to stay and talk to the man in charge. No, he hadn't seen or heard anything suspicious. No, there were no packages left unattended that he'd noticed, and so on.

By the time they let him go, he was in a frenzy, doing his best to look for her in the crowd that by now, was across the street by order of the beat cops corralling the people who'd stayed and gathered.

He went to pull his phone from his back pocket only to realize he'd left it on the table where Melissa, the anxiety-ridden woman, had been sitting. Shit.

He returned to the rear of the building and approached the uniformed officer guarding the bar entrance. "I'm Remy Sterling, the owner and a former NYPD detective. I need to get inside for my phone. It's an emergency." His cell had access to Raven's tracking app and he needed to see where she'd disappeared to.

"Sorry," the officer said, folding his arms across his chest. "No one enters until I get the all clear."

Fuck. Remy didn't blame the guy but he needed to find Raven. Heart racing, he took off at a run, returning to the front and circling the crowd across the street, hoping she was nearby.

When he didn't find her, he pushed his way through the throng of people and scanned everyone he passed. No luck.

After breaking through, he was back on the empty part of the sidewalk.

"Raven!" he yelled, at a loss as to anything else he could do to find her.

She didn't answer nor did she miraculously show up. He caught sight of the security guard who'd been assigned to watch Raven and every move she made.

Remy stalked over to the man. "Where the hell have you been?"

The guard fidgeted, unable to meet Remy's angry glare. "I got a phone call from my wife. My kid was rushed to the hospital and I stepped away for a second so I could take the call and hear her over all the noise."

A muscle throbbed in Remy's temple, the beginning of a painful headache caused by his feeling of impotence. "So you left your post and now the woman you were assigned and paid to watch is missing!" he yelled.

"I'm sorry. It was an emergency—"

"So you don't know where Raven is, do you? You should have had eyes on her the second she stepped outside!"

The man winced, clearly contrite, but Remy didn't give a shit. "You took a call and walked away at the same time we had a bomb scare that in all probability was a setup?" Remy shook his head in disgust. "By tomorrow you'll be out of a fucking job."

He spun around and stalked back across the street in time to see a woman run out of an alleyway, two blocks away. From her black clothes and ponytail, he thought it was Raven. The moment she screamed for help, her voice confirmed it.

As he ran toward her, a man grabbed her ponytail and she tripped, falling onto her knees on the hard concrete, only to be pulled by her hair once more. Remy picked up speed. Before he reached her, a stranger yelled and shoved the man who had to be Lance away from her. He stumbled and fell into the street at the same instant the ambulance, siren on, slammed into him, sending him into the air before he hit the ground and lay motionless.

"Raven!" Remy reached her seconds later and she threw herself into his arms.

"Tell me you're okay," he said into her hair.

She sniffed and tilted her head back to look at him. Red marks marred both sides of her mouth and he gently ran a finger over the bruising, anger welling inside him.

If Lance wasn't already injured and surrounded by police, Remy would be pounding the bastard's head onto the pavement.

"What happened?" he asked quietly, knowing they had just minutes before the police walked over to question her.

She shook her head, obviously not ready to explain, so he ran his hands along her arms to calm her. "It's okay. But you are going to have to talk to the police. We need to get your statement on record before Lance regains consciousness and talks." No doubt the asshole would spin his own tale.

Remy also wanted her cared for by a doctor.

"He's high," Raven said, her teeth chattering, shock obviously setting in. "And he has a gun."

"Couldn't ask for anything better," Remy said. Nothing had gone as planned today but Lance had sealed his own fate. "Are you hurt anywhere else?" he asked.

She shook her head and he took comfort in the fact that she was still fully dressed in her work clothes. She might be traumatized but she hadn't been raped, and for that he was grateful.

"Miss?" A uniformed cop Remy didn't know walked over. "This gentleman said you ran out of the alley screaming and the guy who was hit by the ambulance was chasing you and had a gun."

Remy and Raven glanced at the man who'd saved her and Remy gave him a grateful nod.

"Can you tell me what happened?" the officer asked.

Remy held up a hand. "Can't she get checked out by the paramedics first?"

Beside him, she trembled but said, "I want to get this over with."

Remy glanced at the officer. "Then can you at least get her a damn blanket first? Her teeth are chattering."

The officer inclined his head and extended his arm, gesturing toward the second ambulance with an open back door, and they headed that way.

The female EMT took one look at Raven and ducked into the back, returning with a mylar blanket and wrapping it around Raven's shoulders.

When Raven smiled at the paramedic, Remy was able to breathe for the first time.

He waited beside the ambulance, pacing as Raven had her palms and knees treated by the female EMT with whom she'd bonded.

Garrett arrived and took his place by Remy's side. "You okay?" he asked.

Remy rolled his neck, rubbing the tense muscles with his fingers. "Not sure. Those minutes where I couldn't find her were endless." He hadn't been sure his heart would survive it. "When I saw her running from that bastard…" He shook his head.

"She's tough," Garrett said. "And she's okay."

Remy nodded. His friend had a point. "You'll be the one to question her?"

"Yes." Remy breathed a sigh of relief. At least she would tell her story to someone she knew.

"Remy? Detective Lewis?" Raven called out.

They turned at the same time.

"I'm ready to talk now." She still had the blanket wrapped around her and chills still racked her body. She'd calm down later. Remy would make sure of it.

"You can stay," Garrett said to him. "But you need to let her talk. Since you were a witness, I'll take your statement later." Garrett sat down beside Raven on the back of the ambulance. Her feet dangled off the side and Remy listened as Garrett questioned her, beginning with the bomb scare evacuation and everything that happened after.

As he listened, Remy's hands clenched at his sides and his anger grew until he stormed off to find Lance, only to be pulled back by Zach.

"Looks like I'm just in time," Zach said, his hand on Remy's shoulder.

They watched as the bastard was loaded into an ambulance just like the one that had hit him. Cuffed to the gurney, Lance appeared conscious though Remy didn't know the extent of his injuries. Remy hoped they hurt like hell.

"Let's go," Zach muttered. "You can't go near him without fucking up the case against him."

With a groan, Remy followed his friend to a spot where they could talk alone but one where he could keep an eye on Raven.

"The bar's been cleared," Zach told him. "They'd already done a full sweep when Lance admitted to making the fake call."

Remy nodded. "Good. Hopefully we won't have to do too much PR to get business back to normal. A bomb scare isn't good for the bar."

"We'll be fine. We have a good amount of returning customers." Zach paused in thought. "Add a *Women Drink Free* night and they'll all come back. I'm not worried about the business." He eyed Remy, concern visible in his steady gaze.

"I'm fine," Remy insisted. "Just worried about Raven. Once I get her home everything will be okay," he said, hoping he was right.

Despite dodging a bullet with Lance, she'd been badly shaken and his gut told him she hadn't been as prepared to face her brother as she'd believed herself to be. Even if she *had* saved herself. He was damned proud of her for escaping.

Zach adjusted his leather jacket and eyed him with surprise. "Home, hmm?"

Remy blinked. "What?"

"You do realize that technically, Raven still lives in the apartment above the bar?"

Zach's words were a gut punch. Since she'd moved in, Remy had all but forgotten she was there out of necessity and not choice. "After the attempted break-in, she said she didn't want to go back."

"That was when Lance was out of prison. He violated his parole and we both know calling in a bomb scare means federal charges. Add in the unlicensed gun that a known felon can't lawfully carry and the drugs in his pocket, and he's in deep shit."

"Seriously?" Remy shook his head. "Stupid motherfucker." But he felt his lips tug upward in a grin.

"Keep smiling," Zach said. "The detective who patted him down said the pills look like the synthetic fentanyl they've been tracking."

Remy chuckled. "That bastard is going away for a long time." And if Lance didn't plead guilty, Remy would be in court every day of his trial, no matter how long it took. "At least I can tell Raven she's finally safe."

Comfortable silence fell between them. "I need to

give her time, don't I?" Remy asked.

Zach, who'd lost his first love, then found her again, only to let her go home to Chicago when the threat against her was over, nodded. "Sorry, man. She needs to be ready."

"You did change your mind and go after Hadley," Remy reminded his friend.

"But I gave her the time she needed first."

"Fuck." Remy had wanted Raven in his life for a long time. He'd been patient but that patience had run out.

But Zach was right. Raven had been consistently terrorized by Lance since she was adopted. If she needed to live her life before he asked her for a commitment, he'd have to back off and let her go.

Chapter Twenty-One

RAVEN WOKE UP the next morning in Remy's bed, alone. She didn't panic because he'd held her all night long. A glance at the nightstand told her it was after eleven a.m. She couldn't remember the last time she'd slept so late. Normally, staying in bed was a luxury she didn't afford herself.

But she'd gotten home late, then had to call Caleb and fill him in. His main concern had been for her but she worried about him and how his twin's actions affected him.

She yawned, immediately feeling the pain in her face and back of her head, both reminding her of last night's events. She stilled, letting the episode roll through her mind like a horror movie. Except the ending was anything but.

Raven was free.

Lance wouldn't be bothering her again. No need to worry about what would happen years and years down the road. With any luck, he would screw up while in prison and get even more time added to what was destined to be a decades-long sentence.

Smiling, she stretched, enjoying the last few seconds of what to her, felt like decadence before sitting up and getting out of bed.

Once she was in the bathroom, she finished up her morning routine, and a thought struck. One she'd never considered because she'd never believed Lance would truly be out of her life. Being free meant she could go where she wanted. Do what she desired. Live wherever she chose. Tears filled her eyes at the thought. To Raven, that was real luxury.

The question remained, how did she want to define her new life?

Footsteps in the bedroom jarred her out of her thoughts. She wiped her eyes, opened the door, and joined Remy in the other room where he was setting his iPad on the charger.

"Morning," she said.

He stood tall, facing her. "Morning. How are you feeling?"

Surprised by the urge but unable to control it, she grinned. "Like a million bucks." For a woman on a bar manager's salary, she couldn't help but laugh at her words.

His lips curved upward. "Good. No residual pain or headache?"

She catalogued her minor injuries. Her knees were raw and bandaged, her palms hurt from where she'd hit the pavement, and sure, her face and head hurt.

She still felt amazing. "Nothing I can't handle," she assured him.

"Good." He shoved his hands into his jeans pocket.

She walked to him and tipped her head, meeting his gaze. "How about you? How are you feeling?"

"Sometimes it feels like my adrenaline is still running strong. Looking for you and not being able to find you took twenty years off my life."

She couldn't imagine his fear. "I'm so sorry. I was searching for you when Lance found me."

"Not your fault. Even I have to admit that bomb threat phone call was pretty smart." His self-deprecating smile didn't reach his eyes. "He outsmarted me. On the positive side, I called Garret this morning for an update since the hospital won't give me any information."

"And?" She held her breath.

"Some broken ribs, a fractured leg, but no internal injuries. The bastard's been arrested for a host of charges, many of them federal. Let's just say no matter who his mother hires to represent him, he's screwed."

She let out a long breath. "Good." Though she'd figured as much, it helped to hear Remy assure her it was true.

His cell rang, interrupting them. He pulled it out of his pocket, glanced at the screen, then put the phone to his ear. "Hello?" He listened and said, "Send him up. Thanks." He disconnected the call. "Caleb is here."

She nodded. "He didn't mention coming by but I know he was worried."

"Can't say I blame him," Remy said. "I'd want to see you in person, too."

They met him at the elevator and he stepped inside the apartment, immediately pulling her into a long hug. She returned the gesture. This was her family. Caleb and Owen. And she was damn lucky to have them both.

He released her and she stepped back, waiting as the two men in her life shook hands.

"I need to hear what happened last night," he said.

Raven glanced at Remy and they exchanged, what she thought, was silent dialogue.

I don't want to talk about the details and relive it, she thought.

But he's your brother and deserves to know. Remy's golden eyes held hers.

"Sure," she murmured to Caleb. "Can I get you a cup of coffee?" she offered. Stalling.

He shook his head.

"Why don't you two go talk in the living room?" Remy suggested. "I'm going to go take care of some things in my office. Give you two time alone."

Caleb shot him a grateful glance, then wrapped an arm around her shoulders. Together they walked to the big room and took seats on the sofa.

She curled a leg beneath her, facing him. "Don't you have to work today?" she asked.

"Took the day off when you called and before you give me a hard time, don't argue about it. It's fine. I'm a partner, remember?"

She grinned. "Did I ever tell you how proud I am of you? My brother, the real estate mogul."

Instead of smiling back, a crease formed between his eyebrows. "Is it that hard to talk about?"

Her shoulders slumped at being caught deflecting. "It's the reliving it. For all my pushing to make myself bait... I wasn't as prepared as I thought."

"Hey. Are you kidding? You are here, alive, un-hurt... for the most part." He ran a finger over the bruises on her cheek she'd seen in the mirror earlier. "I'd say you handled yourself and Lance just right." He winced as he said his twin's name. "But I'll give you a break and go first. There's another reason I didn't go into the office."

"Lance," she murmured. Because... what else?

He blew out a rough breath and nodded. "I agreed to go with Mom to see Lance at the precinct."

She leaned forward, covering his hand with hers. No way would she be angry with him for being there for his mother or sibling.

"I understand," she told him. "Lance isn't just your brother, he's your twin." As much as she loved Caleb, she'd always known there was a chance that one day, Lance would get to him. Make him feel guilty and…

"Hey." Caleb's voice interrupted her flow of thought. "Whatever you're thinking, that's not it. I'm with *you*, Raven. I always told you that. I told Lance he was dead to me." He dipped his head and his voice was sad and resigned.

She gasped. "You did that for me?"

"I did it for all of us. You, me, and Owen." *Especially Owen.*

Raven heard the words he didn't say and that, she understood. He needed to protect his precious boy. But she was still shocked. For all Lance had done in the past, Caleb hadn't cut his brother off. He might not have spoken to him that she knew of, but the connection, the relationship, had existed. Apparently, no longer.

"What about… Mom? I mean, Cassandra?" Old habits died hard, Raven supposed. The woman had raised her, after all. "I'm sure she pressured you to stand by your brother and turn your back on me."

In fact, Raven assumed she'd be hearing from Cassandra very soon and she'd find a way to twist last night and blame it on her.

"Mom tried but I laid down the law. If she wants to see her grandson, she needs to lay off you. No contact, no threats, nothing."

Raven parted her lips as Caleb dealt yet another surprise. "You did that for me?"

"I did one better." A soft smile lifted his lips. "I told her that she couldn't support Lance, not with a lawyer or any other way. He's a sociopath who deserves to rot in jail. If I find out otherwise, she's out of mine and Owen's life. For good."

As his words settled, Raven studied him, the bloodshot eyes and sorrowful lines around his mouth. They'd pass and he'd be happy again. She intended to make certain of it.

"Did she agree?"

He answered with a curt nod of his head. "I said it all in front of Lance and she walked out of the room beside me. I watched her get into her car."

Wow. "Are you okay?" she asked.

"I am. I can't even say I love my brother because he tormented anyone in his vicinity from the time we were little."

Yes, he had, she thought, feeling worse for Caleb than she did for herself.

"Your turn."

After all he'd said and done, she drew a deep breath and told him last night's story, not surprised when she fell apart doing it. Being held at gunpoint by a man who was capable of such evil and pain had finally caught up with her.

She realized Caleb had pulled her into him and let her sob out her trauma. When she was finished, she wiped her eyes with the hem of her shirt.

"Sorry for losing it." Her eyes burned from crying and now she had a throbbing ache in her temple.

Caleb frowned. "I'll ignore that apology. You have every right to be an emotional mess."

She treated him to a grim smile.

A few moments of easy silence passed until Caleb spoke again. "So? What are your plans now that you're free?"

"I thought about that earlier. Being free to make my own choices about where I'll go, live, what I really want to do with my life." Though she hadn't answered those questions earlier, she knew the answers.

"And?"

She lifted her shoulder in a little shrug. "I choose Remy, whatever that means." He loved her and she'd never said it back. He'd helped her, given her shelter in more ways than a roof over her head, and she owed it to Remy, and herself, to be honest about her feelings for him. She could do that now, without the worry of any repercussions.

Caleb grinned. "It means happiness, Raven. Now

go and live the life you've always deserved."

She planned to do exactly that.

REMY HADN'T MEANT to eavesdrop but he'd stepped out of the office with the intention of going to his bedroom when their voices carried.

I choose Remy.

His heart beat a rapid staccato in his chest as she said the words he'd been hoping to hear for too long. He heard the sound of footsteps and Raven walking her brother out.

He joined them in the foyer by the elevator and exchanged a few words with Caleb before the doors opened. The siblings hugged with promises to get together for their weekly dinner with Owen on Wednesday.

Raven turned to Remy, an easy, relaxed smile on her face. One he'd never seen before. "We're free that night, right?"

She was automatically including him in her family dinner. Not because he was her security or protection but because... he was one of them and she wanted him there.

"Yeah, baby. We're free."

Caleb stepped onto the lift. "Take care of my sister," he said as the doors shut, leaving them alone.

Remy glanced at Raven and held out his arms, catching her as she jumped into his embrace, spider monkey style. He wrapped his arms around her and walked through the penthouse, heading for the bedroom, where he planned to lower her to the bed.

Instead, she held on tight. "I need to tell you something," she said softly.

"I'm listening."

Her arms still wrapped around his neck, she leaned back and looked into his eyes. "I realized something this morning."

"What's that?"

"I'm free to do anything I want. Go anywhere, do anything. Love anyone without fear of them or the people they care about being hurt."

He waited, heart pounding, as she spoke. "And I love you, Remington Sterling."

He'd been waiting too damn long for those words and now that she'd said them, she was his. He was never letting her go.

"I love you, too, Raven Walsh."

Someday Sterling, he thought. But there was time and wasn't that the beauty of this new day? With that in mind, he pressed his lips to hers and she melted into him, as the kiss went on.

Eventually, he laid her on the bed, undressed her,

and made love to the woman he intended to keep in his home and his heart. Forever, he thought, that one word settling in his soul.

Epilogue

Six Months Later

RAVEN JOINED REMY'S family as they gathered at his father's home in Brookville. In the warmth of the summer, they were able to barbeque outside by the pool. Lizzie, as usual, was serving and cleaning, two acts that seemed to make her happy despite her unspoken status as Alex's girlfriend. No one used that word because it seemed awkward, and as Remy told her, anything else reminded him that his father had a love life... not something he ever wanted to think about.

A loud shriek broke into her thoughts and she looked toward the pool, where her nephew had jumped into the shallow end of the pool, floaties on his arms, his dad beside him. Ever since she and Remy came out as an official couple, Alex declared her as one of them, and they'd been including her brother and Owen in their impromptu gatherings. Caleb kept one eye on his son as he talked to Dex, who stood beside him in the shallow end of the pool.

Caleb was such an amazing dad and he deserved a good woman. Stevie had expressed interest but it was up to him to choose for himself. As much as Raven adored her friend, and though she'd caught her brother eyeing Stevie a few times, Raven wasn't going to matchmake, though she'd love to see them as a couple.

As for the rest of the family, Raven had been part of them for long enough now that she was able to read the dynamic between them. Thanks to Lizzie's care and dictatorial concern, Alex had recovered from his heart attack. During the one month recuperation time, she'd managed to keep him away from the office, per doctors' orders, allowing him to do some work from home and build his strength back up slowly. The problem was once Alex had been given the okay to return full time, he went back to his normal pace. Nothing anyone said could get through to him and the family was worried about their father.

Jared worked alongside Alex and Aiden had helped during Alex's leave but once he went back to the office, Aiden took off to cover a story in the Middle East. Which meant they had someone else to be concerned about, as the region was currently unstable.

Once Aiden left, Raven noticed Brooklyn had taken his absence the hardest, something she found interesting. She wondered if there was a love story for them somewhere down the road. Or how Fallon would feel about her brother and best friend's relationship, something she didn't think Fallon was aware of.

Remy's sister was a puzzle Raven had yet to solve. A fun, loving woman with artistic talent and business sense but she kept her love life and past relationships to herself. Though she and Raven were close, she never pushed for more than Fallon was willing to tell.

Then there was Dex, former quarterback, soon to sign a broadcasting contract. He'd been courted by multiple networks and was close to nailing down a deal. She wondered if he'd ever settle down. Though he clearly loved women, she'd yet to see him with any female more than once or twice. Remy told her he had the feeling his brother was holding back a story about one special woman. Considering how close those two were, Raven admitted to being curious.

These people were her family. More than her adoptive one ever had been, with the obvious exception of Caleb, of course. Her past pain had brought her to this amazing point and she was forever grateful.

A pair of familiar arms wrapped around her waist and Remy rested his chin on her shoulder. He wore a pair of swim trunks and his warm chest pressed against her back. "What are you doing here all alone?" he asked.

She smiled, though he couldn't see. "Just watching, thinking, and feeling thankful."

He turned her to face him. "Thankful for what?"

"You, your family, and everything I have."

Those golden eyes warmed her heart. "They're your family now, too."

"I know." Hadn't she been thinking the same thing?

"How about we make it official?" Remy asked.

She wrinkled her nose in confusion, only to see him slip a hand into the pocket of his swim trunks and pull out a velvet box.

Her lips parted as shock settled inside her. "What's that?" she asked, though she knew.

He lowered himself to one knee and snapped open the box. "We've been through rough times and now six months of the best times. I would have asked you before but I wanted you to have time to live your life on your terms."

He didn't mention Lance but she knew he was talking about her newfound freedom. By now, the family had caught on to what was happening and came closer.

Ignoring them, Remy continued. "I don't want to wait any longer to make you mine and I thought having those closest to us when I asked you made sense. Raven, will you marry me?"

She nodded, tears filling her eyes and dripping down her face.

"Give me the words," he said, laughing.

"Yes! Yes, I'll marry you."

Grinning, he slipped the rose gold set, pink heart-shaped ring surrounded by a pave diamond halo onto her finger.

It was stunning and perfectly her. She held her hand out to admire his choice. "I love it," she said in a husky voice.

"I picked an opal because it's your birthstone. It's not a diamond because I wanted something unique... like you."

Her breath caught as he pulled her into his arms, sealing the proposal and her agreement with a kiss... that was followed by applause from their family.

"You're mine, Raven. Forever."

Thanks for reading! Next up: A Sterling and a Dare!
Dex Sterling and Samantha Dare's story!

Read JUST ONE MORE DARE

A light, spicy, best friend's little sister/forbidden, contemporary sports romance.

JUST ONE MORE DARE

A runaway bride.
Her older brother's off-limits friend.
Taking one more shot at love should be easy, right?
Not on a dare.

Samantha Dare had one thought when she found out her fiancé was a lyingcheater. Escape. So, she ran from her wedding…straight into the arms of the man who once gave her the hottest kiss of her life. But rebounding with her brother's friend would be a *huge* mistake…wouldn't it?

The last thing Dex Sterling needed was more chaos in his life. Retiring from football and starting over in broadcasting gave him plenty of *that*. But even though Samantha is chaos personified, for some reason, he's *still* not able to keep his mind—or hands—off her...

Is a little bit of forced proximity and a *lot* of sexual chemistry enough to earn them a second chance at happily ever after?

Samantha and Dex are about to find out...

Just One More Dare, book 2 in the Sterling Family series, is a light, spicy, best friend's little sister/forbidden, contemporary sports romance that can be read as a standalone. Download today and get ready to fall for the youngest Dare and the man of her dreams!

For long-time readers: Yes, *that* Samantha Dare! Yes, you will see Ian Dare!

For new to me readers: A stand-alone story of two people with a history of attraction.

Read JUST ONE MORE DARE

Want even more Carly books?

CARLY'S BOOKLIST by Series – visit:
https://www.carlyphillips.com/CPBooklist

Sign up for Carly's Newsletter:
https://www.carlyphillips.com/CPNewsletter

Join Carly's Corner on Facebook:
https://www.carlyphillips.com/CarlysCorner

Carly on Facebook:
https://www.carlyphillips.com/CPFanpage

Carly on Instagram:
https://www.carlyphillips.com/CPInstagram

Carly's Booklist

The Dare Series

Dare to Love Series
Book 1: Dare to Love (Ian & Riley)
Book 2: Dare to Desire (Alex & Madison)
Book 3: Dare to Touch (Dylan & Olivia)
Book 4: Dare to Hold (Scott & Meg)
Book 5: Dare to Rock (Avery & Grey)
Book 6: Dare to Take (Tyler & Ella)
A Very Dare Christmas – Short Story (Ian & Riley)

* *Sienna Dare gets together with Ethan Knight in **The Knight Brothers** (Dare Me Tonight).*

* *Jason Dare gets together with Faith in the **Sexy Series** (More Than Sexy).*

Dare NY Series (NY Dare Cousins)
Book 1: Dare to Surrender (Gabe & Isabelle)
Book 2: Dare to Submit (Decklan & Amanda)
Book 3: Dare to Seduce (Max & Lucy)

The Knight Brothers
Book 1: Take Me Again (Sebastian & Ashley)
Book 2: Take Me Down (Parker & Emily)
Book 3: Dare Me Tonight (Ethan Knight & Sienna Dare)
Novella: Take The Bride (Sierra & Ryder)
Take Me Now – Short Story (Harper & Matt)

The Sexy Series
Book 1: More Than Sexy (Jason Dare & Faith)
Book 2: Twice As Sexy (Tanner & Scarlett)
Book 3: Better Than Sexy (Landon & Vivienne)
Novella: Sexy Love (Shane & Amber)

Dare Nation
Book 1: Dare to Resist (Austin & Quinn)
Book 2: Dare to Tempt (Damon & Evie)
Book 3: Dare to Play (Jaxon & Macy)
Book 4: Dare to Stay (Brandon & Willow)
Novella: Dare to Tease (Hudson & Brianne)

* Paul Dare's sperm donor kids

Kingston Family
Book 1: Just One Night (Linc Kingston & Jordan Greene)
Book 2: Just One Scandal (Chloe Kingston & Beck Daniels)
Book 3: Just One Chance (Xander Kingston & Sasha Keaton)
Book 4: Just One Spark (Dash Kingston & Cassidy Forrester)
Just One Wish (Axel Forrester)
Book 5: Just One Dare (Aurora Kingston & Nick Dare)
Book 6: Just One Kiss

Book 7: Just One Taste

Book 8: Just Another Spark

Book 9: Just One Fling

Book 10: Just One Tease

Sterling Family

Book 1: Just One More Moment

Book 2: Just One More Dare

For the most recent Carly books, visit CARLY'S
BOOKLIST page
www.carlyphillips.com/CPBooklist

Other Indie Series

Billionaire Bad Boys

Book 1: Going Down Easy

Book 2: Going Down Hard

Book 3: Going Down Fast

Book 4: Going In Deep

Going Down Again – Short Story

Hot Heroes Series

Book 1: Touch You Now

Book 2: Hold You Now

Book 3: Need You Now

Book 4: Want You Now

Bodyguard Bad Boys

Book 1: Rock Me

Book 2: Tempt Me

Novella: His To Protect

For the most recent Carly books, visit CARLY'S BOOKLIST page

www.carlyphillips.com/CPBooklist

Carly's Originally Traditionally Published Books

Serendipity Series

Book 1: Serendipity

Book 2: Kismet

Book 3: Destiny

Book 4: Fated

Book 5: Karma

Serendipity's Finest Series

Book 1: Perfect Fit

Book 2: Perfect Fling

Book 3: Perfect Together

Book 4: Perfect Strangers

The Chandler Brothers

Book 1: The Bachelor

Book 2: The Playboy

Book 3: The Heartbreaker

Hot Zone
Book 1: Hot Stuff
Book 2: Hot Number
Book 3: Hot Item
Book 4: Hot Property

Costas Sisters
Book 1: Under the Boardwalk
Book 2: Summer of Love

Lucky Series
Book 1: Lucky Charm
Book 2: Lucky Break
Book 3: Lucky Streak

Bachelor Blogs
Book 1: Kiss Me if You Can
Book 2: Love Me If You Dare

Ty and Hunter
Book 1: Cross My Heart
Book 2: Sealed with a Kiss

Carly Classics (Unexpected Love)
Book 1: The Right Choice
Book 2: Perfect Partners
Book 3: Unexpected Chances
Book 4: Worthy of Love

Carly Classics (The Simply Series)

Book 1: Simply Sinful

Book 2: Simply Scandalous

Book 3: Simply Sensual

Book 4: Body Heat

Book 5: Simply Sexy

For the most recent Carly books, visit CARLY'S BOOKLIST page

www.carlyphillips.com/CPBooklist

Carly's Still Traditionally Published Books

Stand-Alone Books

Brazen

Secret Fantasy

Seduce Me

The Seduction

More Than Words Volume 7 – Compassion Can't Wait

Naughty Under the Mistletoe

Grey's Anatomy 101 Essay

For the most recent Carly books, visit CARLY'S BOOKLIST page

www.carlyphillips.com/CPBooklist

About the Author

NY Times, Wall Street Journal, and USA Today Bestseller, Carly Phillips is the queen of Alpha Heroes, at least according to The Harlequin Junkie Reviewer. Carly married her college sweetheart and lives in Purchase, NY along with her crazy dogs who are featured on her Facebook and Instagram pages. The author of over 75 romance novels, she has raised two incredible daughters and is now an empty nester. Carly's book, The Bachelor, was chosen by Kelly Ripa as her first romance club pick. Carly loves social media and interacting with her readers. Want to keep up with Carly? Sign up for her newsletter and receive TWO FREE books at www.carlyphillips.com.

Printed in the USA
CPSIA information can be obtained
at www.ICGtesting.com
CBHW071824290224
4805CB00002B/2

9 781685 593018